Satsuma Sun-mover

By Adam Green

Illustrations by Carl Slater

Lazy Gramophone
www.lazygramophone.com

Satsuma Sun-mover
Copyright © Adam Green

Illustrations © Carl Slater

All rights reserved
The right to reserve all rights also reserved
The right to reserve the right to reserve all rights also reserved
Oh dear. We appear to be caught in an infinite regress,
and we haven't even reached page two yet

No part of this book may be reproduced in any form by
photocopying or any electrical or mechanical means,
including information storage or retrieval systems,
without permission in writing from both the copyright owner
and the publisher of the book.
Basically, no funny stuff mister.

ISBN
0-9552530-0-4
978-0-9552530-0-3

First published 2006
by Lazy Gramophone Press
Belsize Park, London

Part serialized by *Void Magazine*, New York, USA

Printed by Lightning Source

Praise for Satsuma Sun-mover!

'Like Darwin's global adventures, with a mischievous Eddie Izzard on one shoulder and acid in his earl grey.'

The Telegram

'Falling somewhere between the drawing-room frippery of Oscar Wilde and the exotic frenzies of William Burroughs, this novel attempts to fuse comedy, philosophy and adventure, with varying degrees of failure.'

The Dependent

'Where's the fish?'

Fisherman's Weekly

UNIVERSITY OF CAMBRIDGE
APPLICANT 14450F

Full name:	Theodore Socrates Fintwistle
Weight:	8 stone 4 pounds
Height:	5 ft 8
Date of life start:	06.11.85
School triumphs:	President of Eton Philosophy Club (2001, 2002, 2003)
	Decorated Library Prefect
	Debating Prize – Best Speaker (2002)
	Captain of the School (2003)
A levels:	Ancient Greek – A
	Latin – A
	Philosophy – A
	Linguistic Philology – A

Sporting achievements:
Semi-finalist in Featherweight British Chess Grand Slam (1999).
Non-contact badminton – yellow belt.

Extra-curricular activities:
Prime Minister of the Young Conservatives (2003).
Grade 896 at the portable mandolin.

Hobbies:
Logical philosophy, quietly bathing, reading about fatal diseases and transcribing Bach.

Medical conditions:
Anything without a clear symptom.

Dislikes:
Fanta and misuse of compound adjectives.

My name is Theo Fintwistle. Please give me a place to study Philosophy at Cambridge, for not only am I extremely clever but I am also very good at the mandolin (see 'extra-curricular activities'). I am a well-rounded and refined person. I love stuffy and dense academic discourse and the musty smell of old books. As you can see by my portrait, I am not really cut out for a life of physical labour. I see my role in society principally as a moral and intellectual spokesman. I ride the unicycle at an extremely proficient level and I am also friendly.

For Office Use Only:
Accepted: ✓   **Rejected:**

chapter one

In which the existence of walls is confirmed

'And so in this time of decadence, let us cleave to the bosom of Aristotle like babes suckling upon the milk of logic. Be not dismayed, my fresh-faced flock, by the confusion and ignorance of our modern age. We look around our world and have cause for concern – one need only cast one's eye at Media Studies students to note how many witless simpletons pervade our civilization – yet you people are now embarking on the noblest inquiry of all; wisdom! Enjoy your youth, take ale and dance, but remember that whilst your bodies rot with age the mind shall crystallize like charcoal into diamonds. Rise up and become philosophers, students of the mind and torch-bearers of the spirit!'

There was rapturous applause. Carnations flew, hands clapped so vigorously that some became quite red, and a single cravat was thrown with fervent abandon from the back row. One chap, normally mild and reserved, released a piercing whistle that would have been more in keeping with a crew of sailors in some Morrocan hothouse than a distilled institute of learning like Cambridge. At the front of the audience sat Theo Fintwistle, breathless with a heady combination of inspiration and asthma. Thin as a pencil and pale as a cloud, he was already exhibiting physical attributes that lesser philosophers would take years to acquire.

People chatted excitedly, shaking hands and exchanging nominal pleasantries whilst shuffling their way to the Philosophy Department foyer for welcome tea and cakes. Theo walked alone, quietly savouring Professor Hobble's speech. With relish, he recalled the logical stanzas and the thumping vibrato of Hobble's impassioned delivery, and the youngster knew he had arrived at a place he could call home. Back in Shropshire Theo felt alien to the rustic land and its ruddy folk. His father, a farmer, and his mother, a seamstress, had never understood their son's obsession with books – 'words butter no parsnips' his father always said – yet from the moment Theo won the regional chess championships at the tender age of twelve it was obvious he would enter the world of thought and not action, and that his life would revolve around the pencil and not the potato. He was later offered a scholarship to Eton where he had waited with bated breath for the time when he could finally devote himself to the ivory towers of philosophy and now that he had arrived in that pocket of warmth the world swelled before him like a Californian orange.

The welcome meeting kicked off in the foyer, an ancient square room musty with the dust of centuries. Along green walls there hung portraits of old men looking into the distance severely and holding their spectacles with devastating poise. There were cosy sofas and chairs dotted throughout the room, but not wanting to give the impression of slackness both the new students and their seniors stood erect. Each formed small circles, nibbling honey cake whilst exchanging ideas. Theo wandered from cluster to cluster, quietly stomaching many of the bites and pseudo-sandwiches on offer and pretending to tie up his shoelaces whenever it looked as though a girl was going to talk to him. He had spoken to girls on three seperate occasions in his life and these interactions had been so disastrous that he had since decided to avoid the people altogether. As soon as Professor Hobble arrived Theo made his way over to congratulate him on the speech, but he first had to edge himself into the conversation.

'So there we were, chatting to Chomsky, and he and I were discussing a paper that I had recently written,' said Dr Jasper to a gaggle of his contemporaries – Theo had to support himself with his walking stick upon realizing that this man rubbed shoulders with such lofty stock – 'and Jeffrey comes up and says "Ah, Chommers". I could not believe it! I mean, this is the most important intellectual in the world and Jeffrey refers to him as though he were a dog! Anyway he said "Ah Chommers, I loved your book *Systemo-Functional Grammar*."' Theo chuckled along with the others, since *Systemo-Functional Grammar* was actually written by Chomsky's arch rival, Michael Halliday.

'He is such a half-wit!' hooted postgraduate Dorling Patchy.

'Interestingly,' interjected Professor Geranium, 'I spoke to Chomsky last Tuesday and he said he was planning to write a response to Halliday's book.'

'Saying what?' asked Patchy.

'Well, if I know Chomsky, that old mucker, and I really do – we go way back – and if I know him he would be thinking...'

'What do you mean you and Chomsky go way back? When he came to speak here last year he didn't even know your name!' Patchy questioned.

'Of course he did! He was just being humorous. Ah, Chomsky,' and Geranium smiled, gazing wistfully at the skylight.

'Get on with it then,' said Professor Hobble, in a voice of depth and purpose, for digression was up there with medieval bowel surgery in his list of least favourite things.

'He thought it was muddled,' replied Geranium.

'Did he tell you that?' queried Hobble.

'Not exactly, but he didn't need to. Me and Chomsky are practically brothers.'

'But if he didn't tell you, how do you know?'

'I just know, that's how I know.'

'...circular argument if ever I heard one,' mumbled Patchy into a ginger hob-nob.

'No it isn't!'

'Yes it is!'

'No it isn't!'

'Yes it is!'

'Sorry to interrupt,' said Theo, 'but your conclusion is the same as your premise. That's text-book circularity if you ask me. It's modified into a linear form, but it's circular.'

'The pugnacity!' gasped the nearby Lionel Balfour-Lynn, who then fainted.

'Funny, I don't recall asking you,' sniffed Winiper snottily.

'Say young fellow, what is your name?' asked an impressed Professor Hobble.

'Theo Fintwistle,' he announced proudly, as victor of the duel.

'And how are you finding Cambridge?'

'Very pleasant. I particularly like the vicarage gardens. They make one feel expansive, yet contained.'

'Indeed,' smiled Professor Hobble. 'I always find the grounds here at Cambridge to be organic-looking but not beastly.'

'Precisely!'

'Are your legs alright? You seem a bit young to be donning a walking stick.'

'Oh, they are fine. I use it more to steady myself during periods of intense thought than to aid my mobility.'

'I see.'

'Professor Hobble, I thoroughly enjoyed your speech. Grounding philosophy in the struggles of the modern day is such a bold move, and so lacking from much current discourse.'

'Much obliged. You should come to one of our meetings; 'The Philosophic Realists'. We meet on Wednesdays.'

'Are you mad?' interrupted Bernard Crumble from behind them. 'He's got Transcendental Idealist written all over him. Look at that pale face and fragile smile; too pure for this world. Here are our details,' and he handed Theo a flyer.

'Hang on a second there,' retorted Hobble. 'We should first ask him what his area of interest is.'

'Okay,' conceded Crumble. 'Come on then, what floats your boat?'

'I'm sorry?' queried Theo.

'What greases your engine, you know. What gets your pecker woody?'

'He means which area of philosophy do you enjoy,' advised

Professor Hobble.

'I love formal logic¹' Theo said, 'but I enjoy anything that is dense and sequential.'

'Ah yes,' grinned Professor Hobble, his smile embalming Theo in a light of scholarly approval, 'a rigorous approach. That is what we like to see here. Unfortunately, people like us are almost extinct. We are engaged in a constant battle against the decadent march of the trendy, which reminds me, Bernard. Guess what module Derek has introduced this year?'

'Something with a sociological edge, no doubt,' mumbled Derek.

'Go on, guess!'

'Oh, I couldn't possibly. Tell me!'

'The Philosophy of Sport!' Unable to contain himself, Derek let out one of his legendary guffaws, the reverberations of which once reached China.

'You fuck-wit!' came a shout from a nearby cluster, cutting the jolly-molly like a knife of nastiness. 'Have you completely lost your mind?' Theo was startled.

---

[1] Formal logic involves the translation of arguments into symbols which form a system through which one can establish if they are valid or invalid. An argument that runs 'If it is a blues album, then it is Jonny Lee Hooker' can be compressed into 'If P then Q'. This does away with words and leaves form, which can then be subjected to validity testing techniques which go by names such as Reductio Ad Absurdum (quite a good name for a punk band). It breeds an incisiveness which is great for eliminating grey areas.

Fig. 1 – Life with formal logic   *Fig. 2 – Life without formal logic*

'Don't mind them,' said the Professor. 'They always quarrel.'

Theo looked over and saw two men standing head to head. In the red corner, at twenty-three stone and four pounds, stood Chummy Basket-Water, President of the Logical Positivists and head of department. In the green corner at a lean eleven stone was the snippy young Alfie, the postgraduate head of the Young Hegelians society with a revolutionary zeal but not much in the way of muscle.

They were arguing over the ever-divisive question 'can a man walk through a wall?' to which Alfie claimed 'Yes' and Chummy 'No'. Their chalk and cheese positions should come as no surprise since they came from drastically opposed schools of thought. Basket-Water was an empiricist, believing philosophy should be analytic and that the philosopher's job is to make sure an argument has a valid form and can be tested against the facts of the world. Like all empiricists he believed statements are true or false. If a man says 'All Moldovans love cricket' then a Positivist can test it by booking a RyanAir flight to Moldova and asking each person if they like cricket. If they all say yes, the statement is proven true. If one Moldovan said 'To be honest I'm not that into it. Everyone else is barmy for the game, but it never grabbed me – all that standing around with those big pads on' then the Positivist has proven the statement false. But true or false, the statement is philosophically decent because it can be tested against the factual stuff of the world i.e. Moldovans. Now what the Positivist can't stand is a statement that cannot be true or false, such as 'Pure Being and Pure Nothingness are one and the same' (Hegel). How could that be proven? You could never say 'Oh look, there's a bit of Being and, hang about, there's a bit of Nothingness. God dang it! Aren't they similar? Both beige, both weigh about eight ounces...' The role of the philosopher therefore is to listen to the statements people make and decide whether they can be held up to the facts of the world. If they can't, the Positivist hands them a small red ticket reading 'no'.

Alfie claimed this position was dull and pedantic and that Positivists were nothing more than custodians of grammar, shepherds of syntax and cleaning ladies (though this last parallel was probably made more for the comic implications of them being cleaning ladies than any valuable allegorical light it may have shed). Alfie saw the philosopher as a superhero, crushing woe and blazing like a comet across the firmament of history to overthrow all ideas or systems which degrade or limit the brilliance of mind; his job is to hammer the stuff of the world into the dream of his soul. It was precisely this sense of the supremacy of the human spirit that had led Alfie Forster to believe he could run through a wall.

'The world is a hologram which man can transcend by believing in the power of his mind!' he shouted as their quarrel grew louder and other people started getting involved and waving pencils with menace.

'Shut up!' said Basket-Water. 'The wall is a separate object. What difference does it make how much you believe in yourself?'

'You people are clerks. You are narrowed because you spend all your time buried in dusty old works. You do not vibrate with romantic insurgence, and know nothing of our infinite potential.'

'He's as mad as a cuckoo!' shouted Professor Tuffin.

'So go on,' urged Professor Basket-Water. 'Run through this wall then!'

'Okay, I will,' said Alfie, unfazed by a development which might have made a lesser man pause for thought. 'But I need some time to focus my mind. I feel agitated at the moment and I cannot concentrate.'

'How long do you require?' asked Basket-Water.

'A few days,' said Alfie with alarming conviction.

'Right. Hear ye, everyone. We shall all congregate at Clare Court this Thursday at one p.m. and watch Alfie Forster run through a wall.' There were hoots of derision, the final scraps of food were eaten and the meeting dispersed. Theo turned to continue speaking to Professor Hobble but he had disappeared in the bustle of activity as everyone flooded out of the foyer. Theo sat down on an empty chair in the silence with half-chewed crackers littering the tables and streaks of Dairylea smeared across the floor. He felt saddened that the meeting had descended into such medieval farce.

Over the next week Theo readied himself for his degree, spending many hours adjusting his desk, chair and curtains until they reached his aesthetic ideal. He dusted his bookshelf and became acquainted with the sound levels and ventilation quality in different parts of the library, anticipating three years of study at the end of which he hoped to have acquired precision of mind. He could thus embark on the life of a public intellectual; to be a man of reason and order in these chaotic times and arm himself with philosophical knowledge to conquer ignorance in the world. That was his aim. His contemporaries sadly were more interested in seeing Alfie Forster take on a brick wall. Alfie himself was hardly seen, though ninja music was heard emanating from his study occasionally as he meditated himself into a samurai mind state.

Despite Theo's reluctance to get involved in the squabble, he could not quite resist taking a peek when he saw the crowds milling about on the courtyard that Thursday. He closed Chomsky's *Syntactic Structures* and put on his gloves, heading outside and propping himself up with his walking stick to look over the many heads to see what was happening. Basket-Water was smiling confidently, chatting amiably to people, until at one p.m., with the atmosphere charged in anticipation, he blew a whistle and Alfie emerged from his study in a kung-fu outfit wearing a headband embossed with the Japanese flag. The crowd parted and allowed a straight path to the wall.

'Ladies and Gentlemen,' announced Basket-Water to a hushing audience. 'We are gathered here today to see whether Alfie Forster can run through a wall. So without further ado, let us witness his attempt to do so!' The Young Hegelians clenched their fists and the atmosphere was thick as trifle. Alfie walked towards the wall, broke into a jog and on his approach he began sprinting to the chants of a crowd seized with a sense of possibility. Leaping up to meet his opponent, time froze and the laws of nature were brought into question. He swooped across the abyss of an eternal moment and released a war-cry so packed with conviction that as his body touched the surface one could be forgiven for thinking the universe was about to get caught with its pants down. However if there was a prize biscuit for consistency the universe would probably win it, and his yell was shortly followed by a very unpleasant splatting noise and the collapse of Alfie onto the floor. Basket-Water clapped his hands and said, 'Well, that's settled then,' while the Hegelians ran up to their wounded leader and tried to get his consciousness up and running again.

chapter two
Tension

I

Over the following two years Theo pored over his studies, developing an eye for all the hallmarks of philosophical style (bibliographies, cross-referencing, Latin phrases and a basic inability to answer the question). He studied hard and veered clear of anything ambiguous such as jazz, swing dancing or acupuncture, and instead of drinking and doing the hoochie-koochie he would rise at six every morning to plough through stiff discourse. After one year he developed nicely hunched shoulders which won him the attention of his seniors, and when he started tripping over flat and even surfaces he was ear-marked for great things.

Lecturers welcomed him for fireside chats and soon gave him commissioned work. Chummy Basket-Water, for instance, was approached by a software company and asked to write a clear, incisive computer manual (although logical philosophers are economically pretty useless, they are at least respected in the world of action for their ability to express complex things clearly). Too busy with professional duties, Chummy asked Theo if he wanted the work since Theo's obsession with grammatical accuracy bordered on the maniacal. If somebody said 'I'll try and explain this' instead of the correct 'I'll try to explain this' he would tremble, storm out of the room and flee into the sunset on his unicycle.

Theo accepted Chummy's offer and the subsequent guide caused quite a stir (PC World called it 'a new dawn in instructional coherence'). When Theo walked through the streets his top hat glistened in the sunshine, and he would oftentimes be stopped for autographs. After the publication of further manuals and his thesis, he hoped to be offered a permanent residency at Cambridge whereupon he would travel the world, delivering lectures and settling conflicts near and far.

Yet there were ominous clouds over Cambridge since the conflict of Alfie Forster and Chummy Basket-Water. Their argument did not end at the courtyard that afternoon, though Chummy could be forgiven for feeling it conclusive. On the contrary Alfie, renowned for his tenacity, claimed the only reason he failed to run through the wall was because of the scepticism plaguing the modern age. The presence of cynics at the event drastically dulled the 'insurgence frequency' he claimed, and he even filed a law suit against them, which he won in perhaps the most bizarre case of its kind. Chummy Basket-Water flew into a rage and wrote a stinking letter to *Towards a Higher Brow*, the journal, claiming all Hegelian literature should be boycotted, and did everything in his power to expel Alfie from the institute. Alfie responded by sticking a picture of Pamela Anderson on the noticeboard but superimposing Chummy's face over hers. Two can play at that game, thought Chummy, who then used Alfie's master's thesis to wipe his arse; literally. He had thousands of copies pressed onto toilet paper and installed throughout the department. In response, the Hegelians stole all the chairs shortly before the Positivist's weekly round-robin chess match. Finally, the Positivists did something so amoral to a Hegelian that the details have been omitted on the request of the printers.

II

At two o'clock on Thursday 14th December there was a knock at Theo's study door. At first he did not notice, for he was absorbed in work. Like all undergraduates, he was scheduled to give a talk on a subject of his choosing at the 'end of term' Cambridge feast in five days time. The refusal of the Positivists and Hegelians to be friends gave Theo an opportunity to put his principles into action; to lift his small but confident voice of reason over the conflict and pierce beyond differences. He therefore decided to speak on something rousing, something emotive, to prove that all positions are raindrops from a common cloud, yet he was making slow progress and yet to settle on a topic. He was quite relieved, therefore, to be distracted by Alfie rapping on the door.

They greeted and Alfie entered Theo's study, immediately spotting an Evian bottle full of yellow liquid on the desk – pee. Theo urinated into this bottle several times every morning. Before lunch he would take a break from his work and observe the colour, consistency and volume of the liquid, as well as the pH content, and refer to his *Symptoms of Terminal Illnesses Found in Urine* book. If he was home and dry, he would plot his observations, ranging from 'translucent and forcefully ejected' to 'dark and pungent', and they would join the chart of his pulse and weight on the wall.

'Is that pee?' asked Alfie.

'No,' Theo responded.

'That's pee isn't it? That's urine!' laughed Alfie.

'No. No it's not. Don't be nasty.'

'It's pee, for Christ's sake, how can you deny it?'

'It's not. Why would I have a bottle of pee by my work desk?' Alfie picked it up to smell it.

'Don't do that!' shouted Theo, grabbing it off him.

'Why not? Because it's pee?'

'It's not pee, it's lime cordial, and I don't want you sniffing your grubby nose in it.'

'Drink it, then.'

'What?'

'If it's lime cordial, drink it.'

'No!' shouted Theo.

'Because it's pee?'

'No, just because.'

'Because what?'

'Well, because.'

'Because what?'

'I'm saving it.'

'Come on you weirdo,' Alfie grinned – oh how he liked to tease Theo! – 'let's go for some croquet.'

'Hang on. Let me just change into something more flexible,' said Theo, and he entered his bedroom, searching through his outfits for something casual. While he dressed, Alfie walked around his study noting the thousands of books stacked snugly on the shelves and sheets of paper with Theo's immaculate handwriting piled up in parallel boxes.

'Hello, what's this then?' Alfie asked, gesturing towards two plants sitting on a large turf mat next to which were measuring implements and general laboratory equipment. Theo popped his head round the door. He hated it when people walked around his room and poked their noses into his private life, whether to uncover his health practices or otherwise, but sometimes it was unavoidable.

'It's an experiment that I've been doing,' he announced. 'You know that 'Fatal Diseases' book you lent me?'

'Oh that one. It is any good? I never got time to read it myself.'

'I think it's wonderful. I've read a lot of that kind of stuff and it's head and shoulders above the rest. It is detached and well-written, presenting the facts and letting you make the decision. Anyway, they say in there that tap water is full of pesticides, toxins, chlorine and aluminium salts as well as mercury and sometimes dichlorodiphenyltrichloroethane.'

'Blimey. That stuff can't be good.'

'Common water is a death cocktail, Alfie. That book said it may be responsible for a good deal of diseases these days. But I decided to take a balanced view of it.'

'That's not like you, Theo,' Alfie grinned.

'Yes well, I did an experiment myself. I bought those plants and fed the one on the right with tapwater and the other with mineral water. Pretty startling results, eh?' Alfie looked up close and was shocked at the confirmation.

'Right. Shall we?' said Theo, emerging from his room in his full croquet outfit. Alfie looked up and was speechless. Theo looked magnificent.

They walked towards the pitch on the far side of campus in their croquet boots, Theo wearing an emerald broach to welcome in the yuletide. The two of them had become close friends over the past year, often canoeing together and proof-reading each other's papers, yet their friendship was straining with the cold war because Theo was a member of both societies. He was obliged to join the Positivists since Chummy's department paid for his scholarship, yet his personal affiliations with Alfie meant he felt rotten not attending the Hegelian meetings. Now that the societies were in conflict, he would be forced to take sides and there was no better time than membership renewal before the feast.

There was a palpable tension in the air as they strolled, for after the normal bit of introductory 'so, how are things?' frippery, the serious issue worked itself to the fore with the logic of a domino and Theo feared the discussion. He was so disappointed that the two sides had collapsed into quarrelling that he was not keen on renewing his membership to either. It was only a matter of time before Alfie asked him what his plans were and though they played the first round peacefully enough, it was when Theo knocked off for the second hoop that Alfie casually said, 'So we haven't received your membership forms for next semester, Theo.'

'I know,' he mumbled.

'I mean, I realize everyone is busy, but, well, you know how Percy likes to get things sorted nice and early.'

'Yes,' he mumbled more quietly.

'You are planning to renew your membership, aren't you?' Alfie asked. There was a pause.

'I'm not sure,' Theo said. Alfie stood tall and rested his croquet stick against his thigh in an expression that was assured yet concerned. 'Look, Alfie, I know what you're thinking. Gosh, you've been a great friend these past two years, but all this nastiness between you and the Positivists has really unsettled me and,' he took a deep breath, 'I don't feel either of you have attained the unified truth.'

'What are you talking about?'

'I want to uncover unity,' Theo stated, putting his croquet stick down and clasping his hands together to form an indestructible mandala.

'What do you mean by that?'

'We must find the architecture which envelopes all thoughts. The fact that you two societies are arguing means neither of you have found that architecture. If you had, there would be no argument.'

'The argument will be over as soon as I run through that wall.'

'You're not going to try it again are you?' queried Theo.

'I feel confident that so long as the crowd consists only of Hegelians I will make it past the wall this time.'

'Alfie I must discourage you,' said Theo severely.

'I can do it, Theo. Have you no faith?'

'I have faith in you to an extent, but I would hate for you to fail. You made a bit of a fool of yourself last time and I don't think it did your position much good. Besides, what is all this awful one-upmanship?'

'So you believe the Positivists? You think matter stands over mind?'

'I am not a Positivist. I believe we should see philosophy as a means of changing the world, and I disagree with their myopia. But I also believe that things like walls are basically obstacles.'

'If you really believe philosophy can change the world, you should leave those guys.'

'It's not that simple. If I leave them I'll lose my scholarship.'

'So is that what this is about? I thought you were a philosopher, not a business man!'

'I am, but man needs bread for the stomach as well as the mind.'

'Theo you are hardly going to starve if you lose your scholarship!'

'No. But there are other fundamental necessities that I will not be able to provide for.'

'Like what?'

'Take my clothes, for instance. Ordinary washing machines cannot clean my outfits. I have to take them to a specialist woman called Doris Blossom who lives in Dover and charges extortionate prices. If I lost my scholarship I would never be able to wash my clothes properly, and that is an eventuality that I am just not willing to risk.'

'I think you are losing perspective, Theo. Who gives a fiddle about your clothes?'

'I do,' he said. It wasn't the full truth of course. There was a woman called Doris Blossom and she did charge a lot of money, and losing his scholarship would demand more earthy clothes, but Theo had come far enough to meet personal sacrifice head on. Rather, he wanted to avoid having to explain to Alfie that he did subscribe to certain elements of Positivist thought, such as their demand for rigour. There was a silence about the length of a pole vault at the end of which Alfie decided to back off a little.

'Just think about it, Theo. I don't want this to drive a wedge between us, so I won't push you.'

'Thank you, Alfie,' said Theo and Alfie smiled, cupping his hand gently against Theo's member, but Theo pulled back as if to say 'I'm not sure about that stuff, Alfie'. The match ended up a draw, they embraced and Theo unicycled home, stopping by a public house on the way. Feeling tense about the vote as well as these frequent and unwanted homosexual advances, he approached the Tally-Ho. Up on the front wall was a sign reading 'No Dogs or Hegelians'. It seemed that Cambridge itself had now been split down the middle, as every Tom, Dick and Harry was claiming their allegiance even if they had nothing to do with the Philosophy Department. Some cafés and restaurants sided with the Positivists and refused entry to Hegelians, or if they let them in they would normally violate their food. The petrol stations, post offices and public transportation systems had sided with the Hegelians, and often refused to serve the Positivists (buses were known to wait for a Positivist to run to the stop, and then just as he reached the bus door, pull away). The Tally-Ho, needless to say, was firmly entrenched in the Positivist camp, and as Theo neared the door a large bouncer in a black bomber jacket stood with his arms folded looking pugnacious. Theo looked up at him, and there was a pause.

'No 'egelians in 'ere mate.'

'Sorry?' said Theo.

'You 'eard me, no 'egelians in 'ere. See that sign? That means no – foockin' – 'egelians.'

'I am not a Hegelian!' asserted Theo.

'Yes you fooking are. I know your sort, I don't want your poofy, nancy rubbish in here. This is a bona fide, Positivist pub, awright? For men. So just fook off.'

'Eloquently put.'

'Oh, let him in. He's with us,' said Berty, one of Chummy's sidekicks.

'What? I just saw him wiv Alfie that other Hegelian!'

'Awesome powers of deduction,' mumbled Theo.

'He's fine. He's a floating voter.'

'Never mind. All I wanted was an orange juice,' and he turned to walk off.

'I suggest you move to Rio, Feo,' shouted the bouncer.

chapter three

The Quest for Unity

After his morning arm exercises Theo headed through the smooth path that leads past Clare College, and as he reached the library he paused a moment to behold the majestic temple of knowledge with tables, chairs and words casting a fearsome shadow over the adjacent fields. Suitably inspired, he entered that citadel as the rush of power flooded in via the dusty smell of weight and thought, and he walked up two flights of stairs to the South Wing. He normally did his reading in the Music section. The Philosophy section did not inspire him; it had a grotty door and the view was drab. In the Music section, however, he was elevated. The rich, blue carpet was so soft and fluffy that it made one want to take off one's trousers and rub one's bottom against it, while the oaken, carved shelves were soil brown. He had also found a special chair which he particularly enjoyed because it was soft yet not luxurious, and when you leant back it was supportive without being unpleasantly hard. So it was here, in this darkened and lonely spot, that Theo Fintwistle hoped to find a royal idea to base his speech on, something to transcend the splintered factions.

It is generally agreed that finding the unity of the universe is fiendishly tricky. Some claim you have to view the cosmos from a telescope of infinite distance and see existence sprawled in one macro sense, while others believe you should search for it in the small, the subatomic. Theo, however, felt that unity should not depend on how you see things, but on how things are. The best way to find that out is to strip the universe of its contents and see what is left, for that would be the glue which sticks everything together. He took out his pencil and drew an empty universe on a page from his academic notebook. It looked like this:

He stared at the page, teasing out the secret. Hiding in that bland sketch was the principle of unity, but Theo could not see any definition. 'If nothingness is the most profound image of the human condition,' Theo mused, 'that doesn't say much for our condition! It doesn't say anything for our condition.' Lost in a meditation upon emptiness several hours passed and Theo did not awaken from his trance until the janitor began clinking his keys and locking up. The library windows closed with a thud and the whirr of the computers died with a vroom and then a fzzz. Theo looked to his desk and sighed, for his pencil lay sharp and poised yet he had failed to make an incision upon the page, and the snowy rectangle tormented him with its purity. How he longed to scratch and tear that deaf mute image with a single thought!

He had not eaten for an age and felt trembly, so he took out his tofu and steamed broccoli sandwich to energize himself for the ride home. The previous evening he prepared it knowing how draining philosophical inquiry can be. It was lucky that he had the foresight to build a five-storey sandwich, the largest and most cohesive one he had attempted so far with an internal architecture that was no small achievement. Theo finished it greedily and wiped his mouth with his handkerchief, packed his bag and left. He got on his unicycle and pedalled the long way home thinking back to the blank page. Perhaps emptiness is unity? An interesting idea but it would not be easy to present a twenty-minute speech about, and he would no doubt be criticized for style over content.

His thoughts were interrupted when he noticed that he was being followed by someone else on a unicycle, a masked figure in a black cape. At first he cuffed himself for being so paranoid, but as he took a left turn here, a right turn there, he realized that he really was being followed. He began to panic and stepped up the pedalling. They too stepped up the pedalling. He crossed the road to the other pavement. They crossed the road to the other pavement. He completely changed direction at the traffic lights. They completely changed direction at the traffic lights, and before long the two of them were involved in a high speed chase to make Steve McQueen catch his breath.

Theo ducked and dived, turned and reversed, for he knew

those streets like the back of his hand – many a night had he paced through them pondering the finer nuances of Kantian metaphysics – and feeling confident in his expertise he tried to veer off the main road and escape the streetlights so that he could disappear in the darkness, but the other fellow was good. Ruddy good. In an attempt to lose him, Theo did what is known in unicycle lingo as an 'under-bounce' which involves using the centrifugal leverage of the vehicle to work it into a bouncing motion, but as he lifted bird-like over the Gothic gates of Downing College he was shocked to see his pursuer rise even more effortlessly and gain ground. Theo swerved past the Parasitology department, winding along the edge of Veterinary Anatomy and round the back of the Museum of Igneous Rocks (ah, many a happy hour). As they reached headier speeds, Theo's unicycle began to make unpromising sounds – squeaks, clicks and tocks – and when the speed increased to a blazing eight miles an hour, the wheel snapped off sending Theo hurtling down a hill and smashing against a maple tree. The caped figure stopped and peered down from the road, and Theo could only see his silhouette against the moonlight. For a few eerie seconds they stared at each other, and then the man cycled off, performing an elaborate shimmy and half-turn the dexterity of which left Theo gasping and reaching for his inhaler.

Theo stumbled up to the road and towards the hospital. They prodded, yanked and squeezed. Everything seemed to be in order but the doctor told him to rest there for the night while they studied the X-ray results. Theo lay back on the green bed and tried listening to the hospital radio station, but they kept playing 'Walking on Sunshine' which became irritating. His spirit was ragged, and despite the doctor's vote of confidence he would sometimes, that night and in the days thereafter, be afflicted by a host of ailments. These included: searing pain in his left kidney, palpitations, tightness of the shin, cramps of the stomach, a fierce pressure in his right testicle and occasionally complete loss of consciousness and death, for several minutes.

When he was discharged from the hospital the reality of the previous night hung over him like a swollen grey cloud with a swollen black eye. The caped figure was a sign that violence was imminent and that it was all too easy to be fooled by the calm, rural air of Cambridge. These moments of malevolence showed that below the surface of order lurked a real and present danger, a danger he had to eliminate in his speech. On returning to his study he sharpened his pencil and racked his brain for a workable title but his concentration was continually broken by constant flashbacks to the chase. His assailant's grace, how he hugged the curbs and replicated Theo's under-bounce without breaking sweat and the simple but devastatingly effective shimmy on departure left Theo feeling hopeless as a unicyclist, a philosopher and as a man. The fusion the caped figure had acquired with his unicycle and the control of his movement represented the elegance Theo had been struggling to find in the library, and he suddenly realized that perhaps unity could be found in the smooth interaction of mind and body. Yes! Oneness is no academic thesis. It involves mind and matter bound in motion.

He therefore decided to find oneness through expressive movement and direct engagement with nature to 'feel' it in a 'soul' sort of way, and so he headed to the local park to develop a sense of harmony. He took deep breaths, made tentative attempts to climb trees and occasionally leapt into the air. This continued for several hours but whilst he made numerous notes and enjoyed the exercise, he failed to find anything concrete. As darkness fell he returned to his room disappointed. He lay back on his bed and massaged his temples with essence of cucumber moisture and after it had sunken in and absorbed he dabbed the surplus off with his handkerchief. William Blake said that the path of excess leads to the palace of wisdom, but Theo was a man of moderation.

By ten p.m. news about Theo's activities in the park reached the head of department and, fearing that the logician was getting pantheist, he took swift action. The thought of rational, rigorous Theo becoming a mystic was horrendous! What would happen to the future of philosophy? While Theo stared gloomily at the ceiling unable to sleep, there was a knock at the door, and before he had adjusted his night cap, it was smashed down with a baseball bat and three men in balaclavas marched into his room. They demanded he come to Chummy Basket-Waters' office but Theo refused, so one of the henchmen lifted Theo up by his underpants so that they cut deep into his bum-crack and squashed his balls. After much yelping, Theo consented and put on his fluffy jacket, and they dragged him across the courtyard and into Chummy Basket-Waters' office where Chummy himself sat with his back turned, stroking a white cat as the pale moonlight streamed across his study. Theo sat down in the dark room which had cobwebs crawling up the windows and portraits of old men in armchairs upon the walls. The fan was broken and the heating turned off.

'How do you know,' came Chummy's voice, 'that you are not... a bee!' He swivelled around quickly as he said 'bee' and stared inquisitively at Theo through his thick, half-moon glasses.

'I guess I don't really,' sighed Theo.

'Oh come on, boy, you're going to have to do better than that!'

'What point are you trying to make?'

'Am I right in assuming that you can be fairly certain you aren't a bee?'

'Yes.'

'Is it your choice?'

'No. I have no say in the matter.'

'Good. Now we've established that you have not lost your cognitive powers, the only question to ask is why you have chosen to associate yourself with a rabble of lunatics subscribing to a world view that is about as coherent as a bobsleigh in a salad bar. Have you been tempted to dirty your mind with the trances of Hegel?'

'No,' said Theo. Chummy nodded at one of the henchmen, who grappled with Theo and pulled out of his jacket pocket *The Trances of Hegel*. As Theo came to look closely at the man, he saw that it was Scottish philosopher David Hume, one of the first philosophers to get really peeved about mysticism. What exactly he was doing in Cambridge hundreds of years after his burial Theo could not fathom, but perhaps some things are so annoying that you can shake off your own death to put an end to them

'Does it contain reasoning?' asked Hume of the book, spittle forming at the edges of his mouth. 'No!' he snapped. 'Does it contain experiment? No! Commit it then to the flames, for it is mere illusion!' He set the book on fire in an act of great symbolism. He then spat at Theo and returned to the graveyard, lying down while elves covered him with soil again.

'Look,' said Theo, intimidated but still confident. 'I really don't see why you people have to be so opposed. It is possible to synthesize the two views.'

'No, it isn't. You cannot dilly-dally around like that. You must assert yourself as a logician or a mystic but not both.'

'Logic alone is too narrow while mysticism is too exuberant. You stare at dust. They gaze at clouds. Neither of you see the world square on.'

'Well, I am not prepared to meet them halfway if that is what you mean. Look, these are conflicting times and no one *wants* war but if it comes to it I'll fight my corner. I haven't spent thirty years in this institute to buckle to a man who claims to walk through walls. And you, you are going to have to take sides here.'

'Why does it matter what I choose?' asked Theo.

Chummy stood up and walked slowly around his office, the wooden floorboards creaking beneath his gold-plated shoes each time he stopped to stand behind Theo and smell his pure, boyish skin.

'We have seen your work over these past two years and it has been nothing short of outstanding. Now we are a strong society but our members are ageing and we need to look to the future, for what the Hegelians lack in understanding they make up for in youth. Their affluent hair, their tight buttocks; we can run them out of town on paper but cannot compete for youth, and that is where you come in. Now why can't you see yourself with us? We're just a bunch of warm friendly bears, really.'

'Kidnapping a man from his own bed is not the behaviour of a warm friendly bear,' said Theo.

'It may be severe but you are not in your right mind. Attending their meetings for two and a half years... how could you be taken in with their buffoonery?' Chummy sat back down and began stroking his cat. 'The Hegelians are deluded, Theo. We pity them. You see, we treat metaphysicians like poor, abandoned dogs. We gradually nurse them back to health and feed them soft, milky foods.'

'Look, if it will put your mind at ease I can promise you I haven't joined them. I think the Hegelians have got serious problems.'

'Really?'

'Yes.'

'Like what?'

'They are over-imaginative for starters. There are so many adjectives flying around at their meetings. I counted 28 at the last session'.

'I heard it normally scales 256,' exclaimed Chummy.

'But look, it's not just about adjectives anyway,' Theo went on.

'Don't get us wrong, Theo. We like adjectives, so long as they are placed sparingly. For instance, during the undergraduate welcome I overheard you say that you thought the gardens here were expansive yet contained; a good and conscientious use of adjectives. I noted it in my journal and predicted you an illustrious future.'

'Look, I am not making myself understood. To take arms would be against my principles. Remember Professor Hobble's speech? He said we philosophers are torch-bearers of the spirit, and that we must go into the world and spread reason and order, not squabble amongst ourselves.'

'You seem to be misunderstanding something,' said Chummy. 'Philosophy demands you strap yourself to a belief come rain or shine. Like a captain of a ship you go down with the vessel if needs be. Like a noble king, the first arrows must prick your breast. If you want to take a bit of this and a bit of that, as though knowledge was some gourmet buffet, then you ought to transfer to the Sociology department.'

'Maybe I just will!' Theo sniped back. Chummy's face glared red, but he took a quick glass of water and regained his composure.

'Look, Mr Fintwistle. If you don't mind me asking, there is something bothering me. You aren't involved in any, ahem, reductive activities, are you?'

'What are they?'

'Reductive monism you know, simplified materialism,' he squirmed uncomfortably. 'Oh for God's sake, sex, boy! Are you involved in any kind of sexual activities?'

'Oh God no, of course not.'

'It's just that, well, I could not help but notice that you have been, well, you have been wearing a lot of frills recently. I wondered whether you were... in love.'

'Frills?'

'Yes, you know, frills, frills around the collar and on the cuff-links.'

'It is to counterpoint the frostiness of Christmas.'

'Well, look,' sighed Chummy, straightening some papers to usher the end of the discussion. 'I'm not going to play games with you all day. Just remember who pays your bills. Dismissed...' and he waved Theo out of his office.

The young philosopher stood up and walked home, saddened and bruised. The sun rose and he stood by a flickering lamp-post to watch it with lonely eyes. Short of breath and with occasional palpitations, Theo watched the warm energy ululating and swarming; a perfect and complete star, so wonderful compared to Theo's complex soul. He wanted to get away from this tension, animosity and uncertainty – to bask in light as opposed to the strained world. He thought about hanging himself, but then decided not to because it would mean he would die. They say that out of sorrow cometh truth, but Theo wished he could just have lots of women at once. He took the rest of the day off, because his kidneys completely packed up for two hours and then his leg went numb and he could not see out of his eyes.

chapter four
The Dogs of War

I

It was Sunday morning. Theo realized that all of his attempts thus far had been too ambitious, and there was no way that he would do in one day what thousands of philosophers had failed to do in two thousand years; to unify opposites. He gave up and decided to stick to his guns by talking about boring old computer manuals, working deep into the night on a neat but by no means ground-breaking paper on the development of computer syntax, which he believed to be the least flammable topic to deliver at this time.

As the morning rolled around, chairs were laid out for the array of internationally renowned lecturers, philosophers and psychologists as Cambridge opened her gates to the most intellectually well-hung nerds of the species for one action-packed day of cerebral assault. At the end there would be an award ceremony for the undergraduate presentations. Egos (and ergos) rose. However, the whole affair would probably rush to its conclusions before it even started. Arthur McWaffle, considered by many to be a pretentious nincompoop, was almost certain to bag the John Locke prize for his allegedly flawless 'Wittgenstein and Paradox'. Edward Foffle-Moffle, the darling of the department, was tipped to win the Academie Prize d'Lacquer. Even the often mocked 'Most Improved Philosopher' prize was either going to Henry Potato, who was dyslexic, or Direnester Voronim, who was Moldovan.

"Men are not gentle creatures who want to be loved and who at most can defend themselves if attacked. They are, on the contrary, creatures among whose instinctual endowments are to be reckoned a powerful share of aggressiveness. As a result, their neighbour is for them not only a potential helper or sexual object, but also someone who tempts him to satisfy his aggression on him, to exploit his capacity to work without compensation, to use him sexually without his consent, to seize his possessions, to humiliate him, to cause him pain, to torture him, to kill him."

Sigmund Freud
Merry Christmas!

Theo headed towards the lecture theatres, twiddling his thumbs and listening in to some other talks, but none of them grabbed his attention. After a break for biscuits and tea, the bell rang and Theo's name was called. He walked to the podium nervously, cleared his throat, shuffled uncomfortably, made sure the overhead projector was functioning and began.

'Fixed point arithmetic, eh, as originally devised by Mackenzie and Turner, is ehm, inadequate for high level computer function,' he shuffled. There was an awkward atmosphere. Everyone could see that he was tense. 'This is because the rounding off and overflow restrictions give false results.' He was getting into a groove now. 'Let operands and results be expressed p and q; if $p=7$ and $q=3$ – in the calculation, we have $t=937.3$ and $x=215.315$ but the result followed, is, eh, 11478.6715 – but we lose the '5' and, erm , the '1, in the traditional rounding off. In floating point arithmetic, numbers become exponents, reducing the total figure to its identical fraction and then multiplying it to restore the full figure. Then we could make it, as you see here on the projector, we record 0.1147867 multiplied by 10 to the power of five, recorded as $1147867E05$.'

'Rigorous,' smiled Geranium from the front row, assuming that Theo's decision to discuss numbers signalled his return to logic. 'Glad to have you back, Theo.'

'I'm not back,' said Theo, trying to keep focused on his talk.

'What is all this number rubbish?' shouted Dwayne Leicester, Hegelian Treasurer. 'I heard you were planning a rousing speech. This is about as interesting as a Positivist's sex life!'

'He is being tongue-in-cheek,' marvelled Percy, Hegelian vice president. 'Pretending to give an earnest talk about complete gibberish! Ah,' he clapped, 'it's post-ironic genius!'

'Are you talking gibberish, Theo?' asked Basket-Water.

'Look, please let me carry on with my talk. I am not talking gibberish. Now, as I was saying mantissas and exponents are—'

'Stop fannying about with mantissas! You are forgetting about the heavy sorrow of the world,' screamed Mark Goodyear, who could be a little crass at the best of times.

'Why don't you let him finish? Are you afraid of something?' questioned Geranium.

'Who asked you, baldie?' shouted Leicester.

'Would someone mind telling me what on earth post-irony is?' queried Professor Hobble.

'You're too fat to hear anything through your fat ears, Fatso,' shouted Percy.

'You see!' marvelled Geranium, throwing his arms up and turning towards the chairman of the floor. 'This is symptomatic of their disruptive behaviour.'

'Eat fucking lead, Geranium!' shouted Freddy Davidson, who bolted upright and cast off his anorak to reveal two automatic rifles. He began spraying bullets across the lecture hall, shattering the windows and pummelling the overhead projector. Theo leapt for cover and the crowd erupted into waves of confused terror. Punches flew, heads were butted and Alfie attempted a flying kick but missed and smashed once again, with eerie symmetry, into a brick wall. Everyone fled from the lecture hall and ran in jagged lines over the courtyard and Theo bolted away on his unicycle.

He returned home and paced fretfully, his head pounding and his legs feeling weak. Due to Freddy's coordination problems no one was injured in the gunfire, but the damage was extensive and the attempt to assassinate Geranium had let loose the bulldogs of everyone's darker nature. Nobody left their homes, the rest of the lectures were cancelled and army tanks moved in to keep the peace.

II

Two days later, locked in his study, Theo began to run low on food supplies. After assessing the risks he decided to return to Shropshire, but with trains and buses allegedly down he would have to unicycle the whole way, which would take approximately five days. He opened the fridge and realized his best option concerning sustenance for the trip was a sandwich containing all the remaining food, since this would be quick to make and easy to fit in his portmanteau. However, a quick 'Food Input' multiplied by 'Distance' over 'Potential Time' calculation revealed that the traditional five-tiered sandwich would be unable to house his vegetable supplies, yet two smaller sandwiches would be risky in case he was mobbed on the way and had to grab one item and flee. The only option was a six-tiered design, but his studies in sandwich architecture had yet to afford him that level of craftsmanship. During a previous attempt, at a workshop in Devon, Theo found that the sextet structure collapsed under the weight or lost its cohesion and even using strips of carrot and cocktail sticks as vertical and horizontal scaffolding could not hold it together. All email and postal systems were down so, crouching by the window to avoid the trajectory of oncoming bullets, he sent a message by homing pigeon No.25B to his alumni at the New York Sandwich Institute asking for advice and requesting prompt reply. The message read:

War erupted STOP need six-storey sandwich to survive STOP please advise STOP

Two days later, while Theo was piling his books against the door for insulation despite being weakened by hunger, homing pigeon No.25B descended through the clouds in a blaze of glory flanked by trumpet-tooting cherubs and a small chamber choir. Theo opened the window eagerly and ushered the heroic bird inside. He took the envelope out of the pigeon's hole and opened it, finding inside a piece of paper decked in frills and colourful ribbons.

The New York Sandwich Institute,
Columbia University,
New York
U.S.A.

Dearest Theo,

It gave us great sorrow to read of your situation. You are a dear member of our organisation and it has been far too long since you honoured us with a visit. Your wonderful sensitivity to our field and insightful contributions to our work have been a source of constant inspiration, and it therefore gives us great honour to be able to assist you in this matter.

By a fortuitous coincidence, this month we are holding our annual Laurence Crustworth Conference, in which every year we explore that rarefied dimension of the field in which he spent so many fruitful years before his tragic descent into madness and death; the Super-Pentarian Structures.

Please accept our invitation to join us, at our expense, as we embark on the next stage of our journey into the turbulent but ever-rewarding sea of knowledge on which the sails of so many great men cracked open, filled by the wind of progress.

We feel confident that with your assistance we shall answer those questions which we all seek, us for our intellectual development and you, regrettably, for your life.

With Warmest Regard,

Douglas Kendal
President

Sandwiched between the pages of the letters, in a somewhat smug gesture perhaps, was a golden British Airways ticket to leave for Columbia University in three days. As an honorary member of the Institute and a man of no small celebrity in certain peripheral circles, Theo could expect occasional generous treatment, but it still came as an exciting surprise to find that he was held in such esteem.

With an all-expenses-paid ticket out of his troubles, he sent the poor pigeon off again, this time with a note to his parents saying he was taking a research sabbatical and would contact them soon.

III

When the evening of his departure arrived he donned his moleskin overcoat and unicycled past the thatched huts and sandy bricks of his college town towards Stansted Airport, an eight-hour journey. Tearing through the cobbled roads, his socks were sodden with rainwater and his portmanteau bulged with papers. Streets were empty, windows boarded up and occasional strangers hurried and hid their faces. The quads on Emannuel College, normally cropped and smooth, had become scraggly and overgrown. He rolled past them and beyond the sign reading 'You Are Now Leaving Cambridge. Do Come Again, And If You Stole Anything Please Bring It Back Next Time'.

He locked up his unicycle at the airport car park and boarded the plane, enjoying a few simple logic games in his academic notebook while he waited. Moments after take-off, the air hostess brought drinks. The acceleration and freedom made Theo feel rebellious and unhinged, and he ordered a gin and tonic despite never having drunk alcohol before. She poured him a glass and he sipped it. The sharp, citrus flavour excited his taste buds and before he knew it he had gulped the whole lot, feeling the cool diamond liquid fizzing in his belly. He wolfed down the paprika-coated peanuts in one go.

Theo was a whoosh of casino yellow pin-balling towards flashy danger, as his paprika-fuelled imagination dreamed up adventure, perhaps, or maybe romance? The sterile world of Plato would be toppled and replaced with a hotter reality; the freight trains and baseball games he had read about, the sun swollen like a peeled mango and beckoning him to chew sugar cane on the abandoned beaches of Africa, neck back peyote with Indians, win the affections of a Persian princess and wrestle ferocious tigers. How a conference on sandwich structure would lead on to these exotic lands he had not the foggiest notion, but his breast trembled with a Beethoven-like certainty chanting 'Unfold, ye destiny, or I'll bash you!' Unhinged, he set off into the night without a watch or underpants, hoping to grasp the kernel of life with his soft academic hands; hands that would soon be conquering the fifth dimension and releasing the human race like a dove.

chapter five

New York/
To That Tall Skyline I Come/
Flying in From Stansted/
To Your Door

He was still drunk nine hours later when nearing America. The airplane cut through the clouds into the Manhattan skyline and the sun poured through the aperture like fast and yellow wine. The descent was smooth, the deep rumbling of the engine loading Theo with strength as he pressed his face to the window and saw the brash New York rising up silver. The plane bumped onto the runway, screeching at first like a cat moments before it gets crushed into paste by a huge iron rock-crusher, and then slowed to a halt. The doors opened on to a diamond staircase and Theo inhaled, descending with his portmanteau and touching the ground with fervour. He lifted two handfuls of soil from the side of the runway and felt the warm fertility of a promised land. 'America!' he whispered, trembling with awe. 'What dream of opulent exile! How we have longed to reach an age of shiny automobiles, waffle houses, open roads, situation comedies and large-scale baseball games... some distraction from the rain!' He stood up tall wobbling slightly and, lifting a pebble from the mud, he tossed it upwards, towards infinite potential, yet as the pebble curved into the sky a baton swerved counterclockwise into Theo's peripheral vision and he was savagely clubbed by a security guard.

'Motherfucker!' shouted the massive officer as Theo

tumbled to the floor. 'Just what in the god-damn hell are you doing that for?' The shock jolted Theo out of his excitement.

'I beg your pardon?' Theo asked, clutching his head.

'You are under arrest. You have the right to remain silent. Anything that you say can and will be used against you in a court of law,' he ordered, as another security guard emerged behind him.

'This is ridiculous. I was just being symbolic!'

'You were attempting to attack JFK airport, and there ain't no use denying it.' Theo gave a valiant struggle, at which point the other security guard leaned over and zapped him with a stun gun inducing short-term paralysis. They placed him on a stretcher with his portmanteau and sent him to security headquarters where, after a recklessly probal medical examination, he was handcuffed and put in a state prison bus. When he came round his feet were locked to iron rails, his passport missing and his hat irreparably tarnished.

'What in God's name is taking place here?' Theo cried as the doors locked and he tried to shake his hands free from the unpleasantly jagged cuffs, all sense of dizziness and fug disappearing in a snap of fright.

'Don't worry,' sounded the voice of a convict lurking in the darkness. Theo froze, looked up and saw a shifty fellow with dark, short dreadlocks gnarled into an anarchic, subterranean style.

'Who are you?' Theo asked.

'Spinny Jones. And you?'

'Th-Theo Fintwistle. Are you a criminal?'

'Yes.'

'What heinous activities have landed you here? Pray nothing inhuman!'

'I built psychoactive drugs to reopen the inner world, stole high energy physics equipment and sabotaged a covert government operation in the Middle East. What about you?'

'Pebble-throwing,' said Theo sheepishly.

'Ah yes,' nodded Spinny. 'A dying art.'

II

Spinny 'neuro-boy' Jones was conceived when a mystical horseman inseminated a maths teacher in the back seat of a Land Rover during an electric thunderstorm, fusing two rich ancestral lineages in a moment of auspicious collision. From fourth-century Taiwanese astronomers to Shiite Arabs, Swiss bank clerks to Russian aristocrats, Pythagoras to Sitting Buffalo, Spinny's genetic inheritance drew its sources from the cream of our ancestors. If Theo was a neurotic outsider making notes on the root, manifestation and resolution of the fire of Being, then Spinny 'neuro-boy' Jones was the sulphurous smell of the match that was flicked in the first place.

His lungs were made of Egyptian hemp, and his kidneys were squashed sand beans. Instead of testicles he had Mayan conkers and the red in his veins was not blood but cranberry petroleum. Flashing sharp green eyes behind red shades and with torn dungarees covered in paint, he was a man in orbit. His ashen fingertips and stubble gave him a sage, rough quality and his walking sideways in smoke forlorn boots moved the hearts of many a maiden. His thoughts were haphazard and moved strangely, and in their chaotic and drunken waltz collided in colossal conclusion. Stasis was shattered and multicoloured fuzz filled his head sounding rapturous as churchbells yet awful too, like fingernails down blackboards or out-of-tune radio frequencies arguing in German.

Spinny had an unheard-of condition in which freak mercury neurons stretched and criss-crossed around the two hemispheres of his brain unifying them into a throbbing perspective perceiving dodgem images without noting differences. As a consequence he was unable to tie his shoelaces, rarely changed his clothes and often ate rain thinking it was lettuce. He remained unfazed by these limitations, claiming that the segregating, divided thought of the organized, self-dressed man monochromes the cosmic picture.

Since his mind sensed no distinction between up and down or left and right, his career opportunities were limited. On leaving school, Spinny prayed for guidance and one night in a dream he met the ghost of Paracelsus who advised him to study alchemy but surpass the ancients by discovering unity not in gold but dust. He was guided towards three parchment texts in a skip in Ohio and settled in Ithaca to begin work.

After three months, his labours bore fruit. Triumphs included: turning carrot-shavings into toothpaste, milk into pigeon crap and pencil-lead into vitamin C. Later, he transformed a tennis racket into a tennis ball and a stale muffin into Elton John. Some might expect alchemists to turn the mundane into the ethereal, but Spinny had understood Paracelsus' advice and become a new kind of sorcerer – an alchemist with a twist. The mundane is the enigma! The flicker of lampposts and cracks in the pavement is heavy with the divine. Platinum and mercury! Who needs it? There is something intrinsically sincere about huckleberries and foxglove, already golden and unified. By touching the humble, one partakes of this golden sincerity and fuses with the dust. His work instantaneously combined sacred and profane, outer and inner, like one might combine boysenberry with mango, for the soul is a microcosmic smoothie of the universal whole. A piercing thought of wisdom shares its nature with zippy starlight. Melancholy is weaved from moonshine. The swerve of young love is the formation of new galaxies and the wheeze of the aged is the entropy of dying suns.

III

The bus rumbled onwards and there was little news from the drivers. Theo sat in perplexed and frightened silence, biting his nails in panic as he imagined life inside a cell with his future tarred by the sight of grey walls and the threat of buggery. Whilst he tried to remain optimistic, life was not orange. It was a fag-end sort of poo colour. He occasionally made eye contact with Spinny but feared the lunatic might lose his temper and kill him. Theo watched a program on Discovery once about lunatics and recalled that they flip out sometimes and kill people for no reason. He squirmed in fright and asked the drivers if he could sit in the front but they could not hear his plea. No escape! When Spinny saw a rivulet of pee trickle down Theo's corduroy trousers he finally intervened to mollify the philosopher's fears.

'Listen man, there is no need to panic. I ain't going to do anything to you. All my crimes have been for humanity.' Theo stared at him.

'Well then, wh-why are you here?'

'Police found out I was building drugs and gave me an ultimatum: either be killed and stuffed in a box under the White House or take part in a covert operation for the US Government in the Middle East.'

'Drugs! What kind of drugs? Heroin?' Theo asked. Whenever he heard the word 'drugs' he always envisioned people staggering through the night with needles rammed into their eyeballs.

'No. I build drugs that blaze up the soul.'

'How on earth did you get into that line of work?'

'One morning I ate fourteen grams of kava kava and felt a

movement of spirit showing that nature is loaded with forces that awaken the mind out of the habitual grind of mundane thoughts. For two years I worked through the evenings and slept in the days fuelled with magic mushrooms and gin, and my relationship with the universe became one of playfulness instead of retaliation. During this time I studied the impact of chemicals on consciousness to see if I could instil a religious openness to the biosphere.'

'What were you hoping to achieve?' queried Theo.

'To dissolve our local miseries and nudge us back into the big picture. By relaxing strain, I hoped to infuse the population of the Western world with a reverence and light that has been lost after a hundred and fifty years of industry. This reverence would make people sense their inner world so they would no longer be misled by politicians, by the media, but would rely on their own character. I guess I'm a kind of cosmic Chomsky figure.'

'You know Chomsky?' asked Theo.

'Sure. I admire the guy. He calls on the intellect to question and be radical. I use symbols and ecstasy to do the same thing.'

'Yes, I think Chomsky is wonderful too.'

'Yeah, but intellect has to be balanced with exuberance to charge the people with the right vitality.'

'So what covert operation did the police involve you in?' asked the philosopher, feeling more comfortable in the alchemist's presence.

'I was covered in facial hair which, combined with my dark skin, made me look Arabic. I was told to work in the kitchens of an Al-Qaeda training camp and slip tranquillizers in their falafel to mellow the dissent of the Middle East. I joined the camp but didn't spike the food. I wanted the tranquillizers for myself. Anyway, there wouldn't have been much time to try it since the Al-Qaeda training camp immediately ordered some of us back to America. Me and a guy called Ya'zir were sent with bags of anthrax and the blueprints for the water supply of the Western world. In the heat of the desert me and Ya'zir had no politics just hunger, so he turned left and went to Jordan to set up a humus stall and I worked my way back here, was arrested at the border and sent to New York.'

The bus pulled into a gas station and a brash chortle emanated from the petrol boy as he clunked the hose in and chatted to the driver. Spinny became quiet and Theo frowned, trying to understand this strange man and his history, but the thought-filled silence and the gushing sound of petrol was suddenly shattered by a loud cluttering and what sounded like a scuffle. Without windows Theo conjectured that there was some kind of tussle involving weapons. There was shouting and swear words and metal objects clanging against the side of the bus. Spinny seemed unfazed even when moments later the bus sped off and jerked in the opposite direction with a movement implying hijack and disorder. 'Great! What now?' thought Theo. 'Kidnapped by thumb-less Christians and forced to participate in some small town fundamentalist gang-bang?'

Some hours later, after careering at a stomach-churningly high speed, the bus came to an abrupt halt and the back doors opened to reveal neither Guantánamo Bay nor Texas but a leafy town in upstate New York and a fat man shouting 'Hold your applause, please!' He hopped in, chiselled through their handcuffs and foot locks and freed them. Spinny jumped up and slapped him a high five as though they were already acquainted, and Theo dusted down his knees as the three of them stepped out of the van.

'Look here. Do you people mind telling me what on earth is going on? Where are we?'

'Ithaca!' announced Spinny stretching his legs, breathing in and gazing upon the lush trees and waterfalls that pepper the small town.

'And who are you?' Theo asked the fat man.

'This is my pal and accomplice Calvin, who doesn't have an occupation.'

'Please to meet ya!' he shouted, chewing on some tobacco.

'This is our home-town. Calvin hijacked the bus for me and we've won a trip home. Gimme some bacon!' he shouted and they slapped hands again in a gesture of amity. Theo had never felt more hopeless.

'So what now?' asked the philosopher.

'Sorry pal, I suppose you should get fleeing. Do you have a home to go to?' asked Spinny.

'No. In case you hadn't noticed I'm from England.' This was not great news for Spinny. Theo's ponderous physique coupled with his soft, refined air meant that he was not cut out for this kind of thing, and left to his own devices had about as much chance of surviving in the life of a lone fugitive as a wasp in a pint of orange juice.

'Well look man, being on the run is a whole lot better than being in Guantánamo Bay.'

'We are going to be in trouble here,' warned Theo. 'We are criminals now. Fugitives. I read a book about fugitives once. It's no great life, you know.'

'That is just how the cookie has crumbled, buddy,' said Calvin. 'Don't you know anyone in America?'

'Yes. I am on good terms with a number of people at the New York Sandwich Institute.'

'Well that's up the shit-pot,' chuckled Calvin.

'Sorry?'

'You can't go to New York,' said Spinny. 'There will be search parties out for us.'

'I have to go to New York,' Theo stated. 'I came here to go to New York!' Spinny drummed his fingers against his thigh, feeling the weight of responsibility for the smooth-faced Englishman.

'You'll have to dock with us for a while,' he concluded.

'Absolutely not,' responded Theo.

'Well then, I'd sure like to know how you plan to get to New York,' the alchemist said, and Theo realized it was a good point since a quick recollection of his pocket contents reminded him that he had $3.25, half a biscuit and no passport.

'Well then, we shall have to turn ourselves in,' Theo sighed.

'Turn ourselves in heck!' shouted Calvin. Theo stared at the two men, concerned that they were intent on following through with this reckless behaviour.

'So you are actually planning to live on the run?' he asked.

'Yes.'

'And do what exactly?'

'Me and Calvin are going to rewire consciousness and inflate the wrinkled balloon of the modern heart with pink air of love,' announced Spinny.

The words struck a chord in Theo reminding him of Debussy's works for piano. 'Who were these curious rogues?' he wondered, and what accident of fate had thrown him into their company? Theo was intrigued with their exuberance and it was preferable to going solo. He needed all the help he could get.

'Perhaps you are right. I should probably stay with you for a short time,' Theo concluded. 'But just until we sort things out.'

'No squidge!' said Calvin, and they walked to Spinny's lab in a disused shed in the Ithacan woods. The two Americans chatted excitedly. Calvin seemed a nice fellow, benevolently fat with small eyes, loud and accommodating and with hands smeared with oil and petrol from airplane engines or motor equipment that he was tinkering with. He ate roast steaks, laughed a lot, supported the local baseball team and was pals with everyone and although he had a finite reserve of jokes, he made them with such gusto that they were always new. On Sunday afternoons he normally sat in his spongy chair and read the Sports pages over a tankard of beer. You could chat, debate, relay anecdotes and Irish jokes and discuss current affairs and smoke a billion pipes with him for six hours, and not notice a minute passing.

Calvin's occupation was to avoid death and pursue food. To wangle some cash, he tried everything; scheming and plotting with his podgy fingers. One minute he was a waiter, the next he was collecting funds for a 'promising e-business'. Yet whilst he occasionally helped Spinny out of a fix with his ability to overcome important people with wit or force, he had one focus of his own. It involved the leisure phenomenon of paintball, in which men pay good money to run around a forest shooting small pellets of paint at each other. It was whilst reading *An Idiot's Guide to Freud* that Calvin learnt of the psychoanalyst's theory that the two basic impulses which drive humanity are sex and death. Shooting is a form of death, even in the form of paintball. Naked women are a symbol of sex. Calvin decided that he would buy a forest in which men could pay money to shoot naked women. This way, the two basic drives of humanity could be satisfied in one afternoon for just twenty dollars apiece.

IV

Spinny's lab in the disused hut was cramped, a beam of dark wood hanging ominously from the roof and an oil lamp resting on a burnt table. It was crammed with quirky equipment; herb shelves, alembics, electrodes, frazzled wires and a piano concealed under some tarpaulin. His cupboard contained the humble and organic: almond gum, frozen snowberries and apple pips. The most impressive piece of kit was a stolen GeV convulsor worth about $250 million that sends currents of electricity into the brain, and Spinny occasionally administered shocks to himself when he felt like he was getting conservative.

'Okay guys? Now I gotta head into town and buy some paints to camouflage this van. Do you need anything?' asked Calvin.

'Could do with some food,' said Spinny.

'I'm pretty peckish too,' agreed Theo.

'Sure. I'm low on cash so I'll steal you some from the supermarket. I'll leave it for you by the snooker club bins. I don't want to drive around too much in this thing while it ain't disguised. Just give me an hour.'

'Thanks for everything dude,' said Spinny.

'No squidge!' Spinny and Theo entered the battered hut as Calvin departed. The alchemist looked around his lab, wiping the dust from the tabletops, stretching his arms and rolling up a bifter.

'My, what a lot of equipment you have here,' observed Theo. 'I suppose this is the stolen physics machinery. How exactly do you use it all?'

'I use it to rattle the cage of the mind.'

'What exactly do you mean by that?' asked Theo, feeling the revving of his mighty cognitive engine steadily raise the hairs on the backs of his knees to lance level. This conversation was again beginning to remind him of home turf.

'Consciousness begins soft as an earlobe but solidifies. The self is consumed by its attempts to be concrete, defined. To uproot this restriction and open into ambiguous fluidity requires chemical interference.'

'Do you mean... drugs?' said Theo, in a hushed tone,

beginning to suspect that Spinny's turf was not turf at all in the firm and clumpen sense of the word, but was white and fluffy and went the way of the cloud.

'Yep.'

'I'm sorry,' said Theo, his feet firmly planted in the brown soil of the familiar; well-reasoned logic. 'But I like to think that human freedom involves a little more effort than swallowing.'

'Sure. Mere inebriation is for fools. People get drugged because they can't endure the tension of opposites and seek salvation through a dizziness that out-spins the morbid stasis of the relative.' Theo was taken aback by his curious clarity which seemed lucid though contradictory.

'So you do condemn the use of drugs?' Theo asked.

'No. I support them.' Theo looked heavenwards with exasperation.

'How on earth do you rationalize that?'

'Twist-booming of the brain arouses the Spirit, which once awakened draws the material world into accordance with the lines of Beauty.'

'I'm afraid I have no truck with this truffle,' said Theo. 'Having scrambled out of a bloody civil war in the supposed intellectual sanctuary of my nation, to be clubbed almost to death upon entering this free land of yours leads me to question if there really are such scribblings or magic stencils.' Theo felt a little light-headed. There was nothing quite so exhilarating as papping one's opponent with his own metaphor. He allowed Spinny to continue, however, not wanting to kill the mouse just yet.

'Our civilization blunders about, farting on indigenous cultures, and plundering the natural resources of the planet,' Spinny replied. 'The humbling surges of the spirit must be released to re-draft the project and renew our vision. This requires extra boosts of cosmic energy. Imagination generated by the soft rebellion of drugs gives us a fluid perspective so that we can duck and dive, instead of dominate and suppress. To be fluid we need a soul-groover, a twisty boomcutter.'

'How will drugs give us that?'

'The impulse to dream and imagine is our Promethean gift but it finds no support in our mechanical, binary world.

Hallucinogenic drugs lift it back into daylight so the animal root touches the conscious surface and fuses split halves into a unity whose momentum propels the imagination to form a vision many leagues above those that our bespectacled politicians can muster.'

'Sounds like a very wobbly plan though,' said Theo as he paced around, reluctantly intrigued by the aura of certainty around the alchemist. 'Won't drug-use exacerbate an already unstable situation?'

'Better to rush into psychic chaos on a jet ski and find out for myself. Yank the rug away, blow out the cobwebs and see the deepest complex as a web of energy,' Spinny concluded, and after rearranging some of his equipment and pissing in a dark hole in the ground, he turned.

'We know what we have to do,' he said, heading out towards the town centre.

Theo followed him to the snooker club in Ithaca, the alchemist smoking rough cigarettes and wondering how Theo was going to fit into his project when he was obviously such a parochial stiff. Returning him to England was impossible and casting him to the wind unkind, yet he was not suited for the drugs and adventure to come.

They collected the unmarked brown bags at the rear of the snooker club. On the walk back Spinny kept yakking, surveying his options and asking Theo about his life. Theo asked if he would be able to clear everything up the next day and make it to New York, but Spinny warned that he would be ill-advised to return to the public eye just yet. They chomped the fruit and cake from the bags and when they got back Spinny took out two moth-ridden blankets and laid them over the cold floor.

V

The following day Spinny was reflective. Walking across Syria, he had been seized with a vital sense of his own destiny and a feeling that he had wasted too much of his life dabbling. Once he was back he promised himself that he would attempt something global and extend his spiritual vision to the unsteady world. He wanted to build a drug that would seize the mind of man before it destroys itself, a sweep of grace to knock us off our chairs. This would rewire people to the connectivity that glues us together and restart the metaphysical quest for purpose, which has been replaced by a functional but thin atheism based on economics. Man needs a private religion and Spinny would be the catalyst for individual rebirth; an unkempt, freelance herbalist, a Paracelsus of the second industrial revolution, destabilizing the Victorian foundations of our techno-military exile from the embrace of the soil via the juices of our planetary roots. But to work at speed he would need someone to take control of the more logical parts of the work, to plot his findings, hold needles and draw graphs, someone dweebish who gets excited with Venn diagrams and bar charts. Calvin was too libidinous and fun-seeking to be of any use here, and whilst Spinny originally considered Theo to be a burden he was coming to see him as a potential ally. He was sober, restrained and rational where Spinny was wild, instinctive and deranged. Furthermore, Spinny was stuck with him for the time being and ought to integrate him with the project if possible.

'What are your plans?' asked the alchemist, as Theo returned from a walk around the waterfalls wiping the grit from his horse-riding boots.

'Mine? Oh, I don't know really. Everything has gone so cauliflower. I suppose I should try to get to a British Embassy and return to Cambridge. Have you had any ideas yet?'

'I can't see a way to get you back right now,' Spinny sighed, blowing smoke-rings. 'It has been days since the hijack so it's too late to turn ourselves in. There will be pictures of us in the papers so we should probably wait until that calms down before trying to smuggle you back.'

'How long for?' asked Theo

'I would give it about a month.' Theo looked downcast. A month of this living was as far from ideal as black from white.

'My second semester is starting in two weeks,' he sighed. Spinny put his arm around him.

'Don't worry, pal. We'll get you home.'

VI

Over the coming days Theo joined Spinny in the lab while waiting for his criminal profile to fall. Spinny asked him to hold this or blow on that, to twist this and wrench that, to squeeze that and to rub it too, and a partnership began to grow amidst the smoke and sweat. Theo got to classify, measure and record reams of information with a sharp pencil onto neat, straight-lined graphs, which chimed harmoniously with his love of the linear. Meanwhile Spinny got to concentrate on chemical structures as he began his research into which ingredients would qualify for the drug to accelerate human evolution.

How Spinny had missed his desk! Colours bolted and smoke rose from red-hot needles to char the roof. His coarse fingers zoomed with speed and precision from leaf to atom, juggling the elements like a Hendrix of the dust. Chemicals and forces competed for the opus and with ambient eyes Spinny watched that dotted web of electrons, that racing convoy of quarks all bouncing like a thousand Schumacher-sardines with Ferraris for hearts.

After work, Spinny stayed up late smoking heavily and playing the piano. He could not play the piano. He just thwacked it any way he wanted, yodelling and shouting incoherently, the ashtrays overflowing and Theo unable to get a wink of sleep. Sometimes during breaks, the philosopher brushed up on his scales. His playing was rusty, and the neck of the instrument had been slightly damaged by the hurly burly, but when he had five minutes to himself he tinkered with a mandolin reduction of the Flight of the Bumble Bee that he had been working on for some time. If nothing else, it provided a welcome antidote to the unsavoury living conditions. Peeing in a hole, eating mouldy bread and sleeping in the same unpressed clothes were not activities that Theo could stomach without some cultural respite.

Calvin swung by on Friday afternoon in the FBI van, now painted black with a streak of silver lightning along the door. He pulled up, honked and squeezed out of the window and a spotty young man came out of the passenger side; Nils Von Jurgen. An irritating acquaintance of the boys, Nils was a

German hippie who began clinging to Spinny some years previously and, hearing that the alchemist was back in town, asked Calvin if it was true. Calvin felt guilty lying to him because Nils was a somewhat pathetic character. He had tried to become part of the bohemian scene and then realised that there wasn't one. Rejected from most cults and ignorant of politics, he craved the solidarity of a movement but none would take him in. A lone bachelor who shagged watermelons to maintain libidinal equilibrium, he was something of a hermit, but that was through no choice of his own. It was because no one phoned him, and when he went out he usually got beaten up, stripped and thrown in dumpsters. The only thing he had going for him was that he didn't know that he had nothing going for him. Each week he wrote an astrology column for the *Ithaca Times*, which ought to have won an award for its vacuity, in which he tried to emulate Leibniz, Hesse and Goethe in being what the Germans call a 'universal genius'. The fact that he was not a universal genius didn't seem to perturb him much.

'How's-a Theo?' asked Calvin as they entered the hut while Theo was doing his arm exercises.

'Not bad. Still no ideas for my future, though.'

'You been helping Spinny?'

'A little, yes. Just plotting some results.'

'Sure. I always found that stuff too boring.'

'I quite like it actually.'

'Is that my old buddy?' came a voice from the lab, and Spinny emerged in a plume of smoke toasted with DMT and amphetamines, his smile fading a little when he saw Nils.

'Hi Spinny!' said the German enthusiastically.

'Oh. Hi Nils,' he said with disappointment. Nils noted Spinny's dilated pupils and motor-sensory imbalance.

'You are vorking vonce more on ze elixir of life, Spinny?' he asked.

'So is broccoli if it falls into the wrong hands,' Spinny replied, confusing the German.

'Shut the fuck up,' shouted Calvin. 'More importantly, check out the van!'

'Is it finished?' asked Spinny.

'Sure is, punk.' Spinny followed him outside and inspected the vehicle. You would never have known its origins.

'Wanna go for a test-drive? I've put new suspension on and an extra exhaust.'

'Damn straight!' exclaimed Spinny, hopping in.

'Where are you going?' asked Theo.

'I dunno.'

'Do you guys vont to drive to my house?' asked Nils.

'No thanks, Nils,' the three replied in unison.

'I have ample space for you to install all of your scientifical eqvuipment and spare qvuarters for you to sleep in and in which also to enjoy entertainment.'

'No, it's cool man,' said Spinny, although questions had begun to form in his mind about the logistical shortcomings of his cramped pisshole.

'I have also food,' said Nils, in desperation.

'Yes squidge!' said Calvin, and they entered the van and drove to Nils'.

chapter six

The Hub of Unrest

I

Nils lived at number 12 Meadow View, and had never suspected that his benign address would become the seat of the revolution. Unfortunately for him and the Establishment it quickly became apparent to Spinny that this was the perfect platform from which to launch their grand attack on boredom; two bedrooms, one storage cellar, a living room and a kitchen. Of course, some changes would have to be made to attune the place to their wavelengths, ensuring that the sheer vitals (kettle, crisp cupboard) were close at hand whilst the purposeless (washing machine, iron) were out of the way. Calvin put up posters of Angelina Jolie to help their spirits marshall the material world into accordance with the lines of beauty and they began settling in. Three-dimensional lava lamps were erected, and duvets paved the floors, whilst anything bright or with an edge was thrown in the storage cellar. In the front room they built a mini-Pentagon for project meetings out of pillows, stools and coffee tables. Unfortunately, they did not have enough pillows to make it into a Pentagon, so it was more of a Rhombus.

Nils' sitting room would be the lab and they replaced his New Age books with bottles containing curious yellow liquids and strange, dark pickled cucumbers that moved. An ultraviolet laser sat on the hi-fi, and the organic vegetable order forms were soon usurped by top secret Paracelsian documents. Unfortunately there was not much room for Spinny's sensory deprivation tank to lay on the floor so Calvin smashed in the wall and they fitted the tank vertically like a doorway into the void. Nils did not mind all this change and destruction, since their presence in his house meant they liked him, sort of.

With Spinny broke and Theo's $3 now down to 2 cents, Calvin would assume the role of breadwinner, and planned to sell poetic licenses to people who attended a local creative writing course. He would mock up some certificates and tell the aspiring novelists that they could not become published authors without one. At $15 a pop, the income would hopefully take care of food and drink, while his occasional odd jobs fixing wings and engines at the local airfield would bring in sporadic boosts.

II

The house worked a treat. Numerous plug sockets, open space and ambient lighting created an atmosphere conducive to neuro-alchemy and a mere three days of bubbling and smoky glass pipes later, an early draft of the prototype drug was ready. The LSD content was shudderingly high (about seven sugar cubes of liquid acid), the revelation ratio was three per minute and the comedown grotty. It needed a trial run before being released for public consumption, and so Spinny announced that they were throwing what was called a 'mash-up' party.

The phrase 'mash-up party' made Theo shudder. The only one that he had ever attended had been an accident. He had taken the train to Glastonbury once to participate in a one-day mandolin workshop, but when he arrived in the grounds he was somewhat dismayed to find himself amidst a thronging mass of pagans. The whole thing was shocking, there were psychopaths everywhere. Bands, if you could call them that, played apocalyptic music devoid of crotchets or melody and one man was eating fire. Theo had finally managed to barge his way to the Samaritans tent and they gave him a long, rectangular piece of silver foil, which stopped him dying of pneumonia but generated little in the way of heat. The noise, the argy-bargy and the lack of mineral water all upset his psycho-spiritual equilibrium. Many people were sharing cups and the amount of snogging taking place left him aghast. Bitter at the Mandolin Society's failure to inform him that he would be sharing the grounds with 100,000 morons swaying in a group mania reminiscent of the Nuremberg rallies, he became a miserable prat, sitting glumly in the corner with a cup of fizzy apple juice and making derogatory comments about the malintegration of the British transport system. The last straw came when one neolith spilt beer on Theo's piked shoes, and the philosopher lost control. With distressing stabbing sensations in his ribcage, and certain that the festival would never attain a coherent structure, he decided to cut his losses and go home.

'Absolutely not,' said Theo to the suggestion. 'I hate mash-up parties.'

'Theo, calm down,' said Spinny. 'In order to test the compound we require numerous subjects for trial experimentation.'

'But why can't you and Calvin just try it yourselves?'

'This is the future of the species we're talking about, Theo. We need as broad a cross-section of society as possible. And by the way, in order to see whether the compound will be effective against highly logical sequential thought, we are going to need to shank your wagon and monitor your reactions.'

'Shank my what?'

'Give you drugs'

'Drugs! Me! Are you mad? You might as well ask me to grow dreadlocks. That just isn't my area.'

'They aren't as bad as you think. These are home-made, spiritual.' The term 'home-made' made Theo think about his mother and the blueberry waffles she used to cook for him as a child, and the memories that flooded back were warm and comforting, similar to when Proust dipped sponge cake into his tea and was transported back to the soft heat of his infancy.

'What will these things do to me?'

'Pull you out of the darkness, promote the soul to its exultant radiance and make you giggle.' Theo was drawn in to Spinny's charisma more than he would like to admit.

'And then?'

'Not sure. There might be trembling, a sense of despair, but after a sleep of recovery your perception will be permanently healed.' Spinny was selling it well. Theo's life had become unsteady even though he had taken great pains to try to keep his thoughts balanced and ordered. Perhaps this outlandish suggestion might bring the scraggly, disparate chaos of his life into conformity with the lines of Beauty of which Spinny had spoken so highly, and the smell of blueberry waffles was making Theo's eyes water.

'Nothing bad will happen to you under my tutelage, Theo. Take a plunge.' Spinny oozed authority, and Theo's defences were receding. Maybe what he needed really was a cosmic boost, a leap of the soul, a – dare he think it – twisty boomcutter.

'When's the party?' Theo asked quietly, stunned at his own voice and what it was hinting towards.

'There's my cowboy,' grinned Spinny, pulling out a vial of green liquid and handing it to Theo. The philosopher examined the small bottle. What mad plunge into death! Sweat poured down his back, his knees wobbled and the rhythm of his heart would lay Brubeck out with a fever. Ever since he boarded the plane to New York Theo's life had become shot through with stun guns, lawlessness, murder and now drugs. 'For God's sake,' cried his inner logician, 'get away from these unbathed goat worshippers. Think of England, your computer manual career, your hatred of semantic ambiguities!' Yet with his academic future in ruins, his chances of being Conservative Prime Minister dashed and increasingly desperate for some joy amidst all this chaos he imbued the drug with redemptive power. The sound of Calvin bursting up the drive surrounded by people was the final push, and Theo gave in.

'Ah, what the hell,' he sighed. Calvin entered with food, cider, pals and Nils.

'Listen boys,' Spinny said to Theo and Calvin as they huddled in the lounge while the eight others took their own drugs of sorts, three flicker eyelash girls among them. 'We must keep our heads, and remember that this is a scientific experiment. Be rigorous with your experience, take nothing for granted, make plenty of notes and leave the brunette for me.' Though doubtful and panicking as he brought the bottle to his mouth, in the deeper strata of his self Theo saw a wink from the pink flamingo of creative dissent and he swallowed the contents of the vial. As it whooshed down his throat, an ominous chord chimed, and it wasn't the Japanese minimal techno coming out of the hi-fi.

After fifteen minutes, Theo began to notice certain visual oddities. The lamp seemed to be engaging in a throbbing dialogue with the floorboards and when Theo moved his eyes amber stars tagged along, leaving a trail of orange dust in a milky way. He saw the other people begin to experience pleasant feelings and to express their delight by gnashing their teeth, clenching their jaws and rolling their eyes around their heads. Music boomed out of subwoofer speakers, the bass rumbling the spinach and goat's cheese ricotta in Theo's tummy, and suddenly the sensory morphing sensations played second fiddle to an upsurge of animation as the techno music seized Theo's soul.

He had never been a great dancer. He was far too thoughtful and awkward. Classical mandolin playing does not lend itself to physical movement; it brings stillness to the breast. Now, however, he got up and gave it some, thrusting his hips around and making rapid poking motions with his fingers. A bolt of empathy-lightning burst through his consciousness, flooding every crack and cranny; under the sofa, behind the television, round the back of the bike shed and between his toes – cobwebs dusted away with light – the neuro-Establishment usurped by anarchic semi-quavers and immediacy infusing tables and walls.

View became dizzy, jangling like a drunken wind-chime in a four-dimensional banana whirling 'pointy' elation – organic yet crafty-synthetic – and Theo wope his sweat-drenched brow to the dark and rocking beats. Bodies grooved and twirled, and humanity was perfect for a brief moment in the spin of lights, personal boundaries dissolving into one energy field dancing the mashed potato. Perhaps this emotionally charged state could save the species? How elegant this anti-consequence vacuum – a no-gravity patch of space instead of the tangled business tie – imagination and ecstasy rather than mechanical bureaucracy. Touch became close tender, the intellect was busted by benevolent rebels bubbling at yellow velocity, a rise supreme and magnified lights, sounds bended, at the rush bruth-errr you feel very... high, I guess... and you roll ...rolling out of yourself ...slipping and dizzy...formless ... swizzy... a tiny glow surrounded by a slow indigo movement. As refractions of light and sound intersected across a skein of force exchange, Theo was breathless at the depth and scope of his feeling, fusing his isolated pale skin with the neon heat of cosmic electrics.

'Who pushes this round mass safely through the darkness?' he shouted and Calvin said 'I think it's near the bus stop.' The grass grows by itself...

The thrum attracted young passers-by and soon 12 Meadow View housed a sizable shindig. Theo did not notice the new arrivals, lost in deep contemplation of the tiny stars that streamed out of his pinkie with care and tenderness, gathering in small clusters and mischievous formations across the sky. Spinny approached the young Englishman as he was babbling without a care in the world for syntax, flipping like a drunken seal across thoughts like a Hawaiian wave.

Equanimous Spinny:	How is the formula?
Lop-sided Theo:	I'm absolutely toasted!
Equanimous Spinny:	Do you feel more spiritually aware?
Lop-sided Theo:	I feel toasted.
Equanimous Spinny:	Your spiritual warmth is being revealed.
Lop-sided Theo:	Good-o. Well pass that bifter on over before it smoulders into a speck of ash, eh?
Equanimous Spinny:	Stay even, oh logician. Do not abandon reason entirely.
Lop-sided Theo:	Reason can chew my dust. I want to mash myself into a hopeless guacamole of pleasure.
Equanimous Spinny:	Vice or virtue, our great folly is to take sides.

Lop-sided Theo:	But you are using a vice! Need I remind of you of the contents of those vials which we swallowed not an hour ago?
Equanimous Spinny:	Yes, but my ingestions are not to flee misery but to fuel my adventure.
Lop-sided Theo:	But you'd be miserable if you couldn't fuel your adventure.
Equanimous Spinny:	No, I wouldn't.
Lop-sided Theo:	Yes, you would.
Equanimous Spinny:	No, I wouldn't.
Lop-sided Theo:	Yes, you would. For God's sake, pass that bifter before I admonish thee.

Spinny passed it and Theo inhaled in large puffs, watching the coil of smoke whirl from the tip as it shrunk into a soggy black roach. They dwelt in the space around them and waited.

'Did I say that or did I think it?' asked Theo suddenly.

'I think you thought it,' said Spinny.

'Oh.'

'Unless that is what you are asking if you thought or said.'

'Sorry?'

'You did just say "did I say that or did I think it." If that is what you are asking about having said or thought, you said it.'

But Theo was already onto the next thing. Squeezing the pumpy clarity, the philosopher felt calm, moving over to the floor by the radiator and twirling his eyes around his nutty globe-head pontificating all the species that had traversed this theatre, with feuds and deaths; a heart-swaying tapestry of disappointment and larceny. 'Och,' he chuckled to himself. 'Who fights? Dig the firmament dark as eyelashes of night – star powder on dark floor wrapped in scarves of meteors – only a sexual creator could do it – no priest could hold the wheel of this mad dream. Indians say the sound of the universe is Ommm. Actually it is Nggooommmm, because the universe has the shape of a pear-shaped universe. It's very Doppler.' Meanwhile inanimate objects got up, walked around, melted and did whatever the hell they damn well pleased.

'The method for the destruction of suffering is the bending of experience. To know the stray honesty of things is to achieve the final tranquility. The entire universe becomes an extension of your wit, a playground for your fancy.' said Spinny.

'A non-extended monad,' added Theo puffing out smoke rings from a six-inch blunt.

Theo felt minutes had passed since the night began and was shocked when he glanced at his pocket-watch to find that it was almost dawn. Conversations dissipated now and became a series of unconnected mumbles, while the first few tongues of sunlight angled through the curtains with their pale sheen. Theo tried to shake people in order to converse, to share snapshots of beauty and squeeze pink juice of love, but it was closing. Day entered and there was a sense of cross-eyed mush. It was no longer one trans-material energy field, but people staggering with blurred eyes and aching jaws, collapsed in corners, trousers stained with fags and beer; the zing flopped into rubble of smashed hearts reaching out to a flat darkness. The smiley bounce that had once filled the house became flabby and old, as did the once swerving momentum of Theo's thoughts.

He stumbled around gloopy-eyed, feeling weeds and vines growing around his soul and strangling his heart. Red-eyed, his thighs shaking with weakness and his wrists skinny with malnourishment, it was clear that he was crashing back to earth with cloud-stained pajamas.

Everybody else was quickly asleep but Theo was tormented by the archetypal image of the chickpea floating in his mind. He observed its quiet and measured serenity with his jaundiced eyes; cool and sobre, it emanated the steady luminosity that he sorely lacked. He tossed and turned, and there was even thrashing, as he fought a tug of war with the duvet, which wasn't a great thing to war against. It left him feeling unsatisfied, as though he had beaten a small girl at an arm wrestle. He began to wonder if he was breaking down and started hating Calvin for always wearing his Team Ace leather jacket. What was Theo doing here in Ithaca anyway? Soon he remembered about his computer manuals and could not prevent his consciousness flying off into loop-de-loops of three-sided anxieties. He leapt up and started to pack his bags, entered the kitchen, picked up the only plate that was not covered in fag-ash and cider and ate a bowl of coco-pops, or 'Hero Dots of Brown' as they call them in America. Exhaustion overtook his desire to flee and he fell asleep on the table, dreaming again of the no-question realm that is the sun. When the nerve of life stretched painfully, in the collapse of order or at the onset of strife, the idea of light would wash over Theo's furrowed brow.

chapter eight
Firefly Dawn

I

Theo awoke in the afternoon with an empty stomach and a grumbling appendix and stumbled towards the shower. Once he could lather himself with soap the day would soften and the bizarre shape of his life would lose some of its rough edges. He made the dizzy stumble towards water, tripping over a shoe and a body. Hair, limbs and careless love fluids were entwined with cigarette butts, spilt beer and pizza toppings, forming one warm stew of youthful revelry. Theo befuddled his way up the stairs and stared at the bathroom door with baggy eyes. Calvin awoke soon after, peeved at the bodies who had invited themselves to the party, drank the booze, pissed on the floor and were now snoring all over the place.

'Where the hell did all these people come from?' he shouted, having eliminated many of the memory cells which would have otherwise informed him that he invited them. Hung-over, he began kicking people in the ribs until they gathered their things and left.

The shower was not enough to distract Theo from the soft quietude of his consciousness. Everything was pitched in a halo of space and each thought was a cloud in the grey distance. Sensations were in flux, outer and inner waxed and waned and he felt the compressed solitude of snorkelling; fish swim, laughter bounces above, but one is alone. His visual field had recovered little, and things that were on the windowsill still occasionally strayed from the windowsill, despite the absence of a defined third party.

He wandered around the town trying to reconnect himself to reality. Children played in the street with worn down red hoops and plastic yellow swords while their mothers chatted on the pavement resting their elbows on prams. Cars swept past. Two old men with flat caps came out of a convenience store and said 'hello' and one of them snorted residual snot from the top of his nasal passage and swallowed it.

As Theo reached the nearby park he had the feeling that a large truck, making its way wearily across the universe, had finally arrived at its destination and creaked its heavy load to a halt, a few inches behind his head. The parcel was ineffable and basically metaphysical, containing a sensation that matter was simple, flexible and honest. The burgundy carpet of ignorance upon which Theo's pampered feet had walked for so long, which mistook the world for something unremarkable, had been yanked away. Reality no longer loomed as a boring stasis, but as an origami hologram of whimsy. It began to bend, melt and stretch. A bit like this:

A sad warm easy day followed as Theo's sanity pieced itself back together. He stared at his foot and accidentally put a cat in the tumble dryer. There was even a slipper on his head which he put there for a joke but then forgot about. His mind was becoming a bio-emotional scrambled egg simmering over the quiet flame of unemployment. Smoky and ambiguous, he felt inspired to write a light aria but was not convinced that this frame of mind had any connection to the process of saving the world. He felt dislocated and in some way renewed, but that alone was not enough. Calvin meanwhile, a naturally contented animal, was reclining on the sofa watching television in boxer shorts and a dressing gown, shuffling his limbs about and lifting a leg now and then to fart.

'Well good afternoon, fella!' he called to Theo as he stumbled in from his walk. 'How is it?'

'Fuggy. What are you up to?'

'Watching paint dry,' said Calvin, gesturing towards a pop-punk band video on MTV.

'Any programs about Babylonian slave-girls?' asked Theo.

'No,' said Calvin searching down the listings. 'Not today.' They both sighed and reclined.

'This place is looking pretty messy,' said Theo, stretching his legs. 'I think we should clear some of it up before Nils gets back.'

'Hey, come on. Let me teach you a cool game.'

'It doesn't involve risking our lives does it?'

'No, it's very safe. Look,' and he got up and Theo followed him into the kitchen. In the corner there was a sack of potatoes which Nils had travelled to Moorfield Organic Farm to acquire. You could volunteer to work at the farm and in return you took away some of the produce. Nils had gone every day for the past week to gather potatoes, which he considered to be the most satisfying, cheapest and appropriate food for people in their economic and spiritual situation.

'Now, it's one of those games that at first seems pretty stupid. You might look at it and say "what's the point of that?" Because I mean the game don't really have many sides to it, and you can't really win or lose. It is just a simple game that is a kind of release.'

'Well,' said Theo. 'What's the game?'

'It's just this,' said Calvin, who then picked a potato up and hurled it against the kitchen wall so that it smashed into pieces.

'That's it?' asked Theo.

'Yeah. Just throw the potato. I mean, really throw it man. The cool thing about potatoes is that they don't bounce but they smash nicely. They are heavy, but soft. They are the perfect vegetable to throw against a wall.'

'I see.' Theo picked up a potato hesitantly and threw it gently against the wall. So gently, in fact, that it did not quite reach the wall, but landed on the floor.

'Come on, you pansy, throw it!' Theo picked up another one and really threw it this time, and the two of them got into it as Theo too discovered that there is nothing quite like hurling a potato at a wall to release your libido, if it has no other outlet.

'So boys,' came Spinny's voice from behind them, alerted by the noise. 'What did you think of the compound?

'Fun to begin with,' said Calvin turning around, 'but it got fizzy and then twitchy.'

'Were there any religious illuminations for you?'

'Nope.'

'None at all?'

'I felt good towards everyone if that's what you mean.'

'It's a start. Theo?'

'I found it pleasant at first,' he said, putting his potato down. 'I was exhilarated with a kind of sensory ecstasy and very much enjoyed the play of colours and lights but they soon became confusing, tiresome and in the end rather depressing. I do see the world a little differently I suppose, but in terms of saving humanity I don't think this is going to do it. It is too fleeting, random and pleasure-orientated.'

'But pleasure is instinctive and saves us from the abstract, robotic prison of our civilization!' exclaimed Spinny.

'Saving human perception ought to be a more intellectual process. Last night was too physically exuberant.'

'The square of intellect and the wave of pleasure must commingle.'

'Can we really combine sensory pleasure and intellect?' questioned Theo. 'Surely we have to choose. And we must choose intellect. Look at this place. Pleasure leads to an awful mess, clothes everywhere, dirty plates amassing and no letters get posted. It becomes exhausted and leads to destruction. Intellect is the light of our higher faculties and it must fight against the base evils of animal pleasure.'

'There is no war between 'higher' intellect and 'lower' pleasure, because man is one animal. He is confused and restless which he mistakes for a duality, but it is actually because his cells contain serpentine, aquatic, jungle and bird-like forces, because he is built from the compressed remnants of the web of life.'

'But those aquatic and jungle things are worldly. They do not account for the higher matter of mind.'

'The organic fragments of nature may look regular but the mundane is the enigma.'

'You asked for my opinion and I'm telling it to you. We need a more intelligent drug.'

'I agree,' said Calvin. 'And if you want it to be religious well I didn't get any real religious feeling.' Spinny sat down and looked at his notes.

'Perhaps you guys are right. Maybe it needs more work. If we are going to put it in the water supply it has to be in good shape.'

'Put it where? asked Theo.

'In the tap water,' replied Spinny. 'That's the best way to get this stuff out there.'

'You have gone nuts!' cried Theo, whilst Calvin keeled over with laughter.

'What?'

'This is ludicrous.'

'Ludicrous?'

'I mean, dangerous.'

'And tapwater isn't dangerous? That shit is toxic.'

'I thought this was going to be a voluntary thing. That you were going to release this drug on the internet or something.'

'I want to hit the whole nation.'

'It is very ethically contentious,' warned Theo. 'I hate to sound conservative, but, well, you can't just stick psychedelic drugs in tap water. You might kill people, make people go mad.'

'Just see it as short-term intoxication with a view to a deeper purity. Everyone in the streets, the offices, the White House and Downing street, a complete upheaval, the sea of our collective consciousness flowing inwards. Stagnation requires a blitz of lemon-fire.'

'But it seems – very dangerous. I mean, drugs kill people, people take drugs and then, then their life goes to rubble.'

'Are you dead?'

'Me?'

'Yes.'

'No.'

'Has your life gone to rubble?'

'No.'

'Has it stepped up fifty steps?'

'I wouldn't say fifty.'

'So?'

'But that doesn't mean drugs will save the world, because for every person who enjoys it or learns something someone else might be driving a bus.'

'Did you see the light of psyche?'

'Yes, I saw something.'

'Something streets ahead of pedestrian, sobre thought?'

'Yes, but it didn't last and besides that isn't the point. The point is the effect it may have on people.'

'No one will go mad. I'm going to build a smart drug.'

'How do we get the drugs into the water?' asked Calvin, who found the idea amusing, which was enough justification for him. Spinny pulled out a large portfolio.

'I was sent back from Afghanistan with instructions to 'kill the infidels' by putting anthrax in the tap water and they gave me this folder with the blueprints for the water-supply stations of the United States. Now I don't sympathize with Al Qaeda's goal of destruction but I'm interested in mellowing the Western superstructure for safety reasons.'

'What reasons are they?' asked Theo

'Our cultural dominance is blowing out the candles of indigenous and distant peoples. At the same time the symbols and currency of our language, the golden arches of McDonald's, stem from a psychologically static people whose rejection of the metaphysical leaves them unequipped to represent in their daily ideology the subconscious, which is the fountain of religious feeling. Now when I say religious feeling I don't mean bishops and Bibles. I mean the strange ecstatic mist that hangs over the heart.'

'But what exactly do you mean by 'mellow the Western superstructure?'

'A capitalist-industrial monster has a status that appears dominant but could be dismantled. We could do this by anchoring a programme for regeneration in the collective, creative mind. Put science, politics and weaponry back under our thumb and squash this fragmented dirty bomb of the global state into a ball of workable clay again. At the moment it is unsteady. Our culture needs to climb down. It needs awe. To do this we must touch upon the nerve at the base of the unconscious. Only this universal impulse will allow our lives to run together and the way to hit the nerve big is to do it covert, via water.'

II

Over the next three weeks Spinny handed out more developed drugs and they were improving. Calvin gobbled them up greedily and gave 'yay or nay' feedback while Theo, so reluctant at first to dabble, began taking a curious interest. If the original drug was a first draft perhaps it could evolve into a valuable experience. There was no denying a profundity in his experience. It had flaws, but it was newborn. The second drug was more cohesive and refined and the third permanently transformed elements of Theo's perception. For instance, the day after drug three, when he looked at inanimate objects, he felt them breathing. This was a permanent element of his interpretation of the world and made him feel at one with the cosmos; a concrete sensation, a door opened by drugs, and enough to make Theo pursue this form of development. He was occasionally seized with moments of woe, of course, at the recollection of his life at Cambridge and the questions they must be asking, if the place hadn't been levelled by tanks, but for the most part his focus remained on the present.

Windows stayed shut. People crossed in the hallway and made primitive grunts of communication, ominous odours wafted through the house in a miasma of rot and an umbrella was found smouldering in the oven. Calvin occasionally painted giant paeans to the body on the walls; breasts heavy like melons, vaginas with lightning rocketing out and cherubs pointing trumpets towards storming penises that clashed like swords over hills of bottoms. He wasn't an artist by any stretch, but paganism is paganism. Let's not get hung up on technicalities.

The three of them smoked cigarettes, sniffed powders and stuck pills up their bums to expand their consciousnesses in the search for the opus and in the weeks that followed, 12 Meadow View turned into an ancient think-tank, full of groaning and wisdom. The place was intolerably stinky, but something significant was happening. Rather than feeding the machine civilization of economics and business, they were withdrawing into a majestic inner kingdom, unleashing the rich history of their collective unconscious which flooded out into sprawling, shocking drawings and mythical sketches; electric poems, the scattering of mental particles and rumbling vitality.

It was all very inward and misty and quite a change to Theo. Whereas he had once lived in the flat dimension of the input-output world comprising logic, tax and politics, Spinny pointed to a language of a higher order. Organisation of culture and civilisation would not be gained through clear thinking alone, Theo was discovering, but via the leaps and strides of the subconscious, which propels the human imagination further than the pitiful two dimensions of sobriety. That paltry scene no longer seemed like home now that their minds had become inflamed, and with chutzpah they believed the world could be flipped, melted and fashioned anew. Their fiery anarchism would turn boredom into toffee and their simmering bodies would drive back the tank of techno-military industrialism into the grave of David Hume.

III

Spinny refined the compound over multiple incarnations and in the process came to realize the limitations of his initial vision. Rather than blazing into the brain with explosions and rockets he needed to try something quieter. Theo's point that a destruction of sanity would lead to anarchy and collapse had struck home, and Spinny realized that a subtle nod towards the deep heat and wisdom at the depth of mind would inspire a silent revolution; beautiful and no less sweeping. What he required, therefore, were sad cuttings of humble life, not Big Bangs. The compound had to embalm the nervous psyche like sugared butter. It should sooth and unravel like Chet Baker and Perry Como in fluffy Swedish jumpers humming 'My Funny Valentine' by a chestnut-roasting fire, supported by the mellifluous tones of a vintage Rhodes and the soft gongs of warm bells being licked by Marilyn Monroe.

Whilst this change of heart was essential for the development of the project, it left Spinny in a crisis. In his travels he always collected samples that were violent, acidic and sudden in their effect on consciousness. Now that he was using a softer lens he sought new ingredients, like palm honey and bancha twigs. After two weeks of painstaking research, he found that the lands where such ingredients could be found were impossibly distant, given that poverty, lack of time and an FBI campaign to end his life rendered international travel impossible.

'Problem,' he sighed over a toast dinner with Theo, while Calvin was out exercising his libido in a local discotheque and Nils was away on a lymph-node purification retreat.

'What is it?' asked Theo.

'I'm toning the opus down to create a transformation that won't make people go mad, so I am scouting for new ingredients; fragments and cuttings of the cosmos... ordinary juices, roots and sandals. I have numerous samples but there are three places where I know the forces of life are strongest. One is in West Africa – Ghana. Secondly, a small island in the Pacific, a place I have always dreamed of visiting because of the legendary quality of its kava kava but never got round to it. And lastly, the coast of Spain, in what used to be Josho Giyera, a million years ago, now Barcelona.'

'Nice destinations,' said Theo. 'How are you going to get there?'

'This is the problem. I can't.'

'That is a problem,' agreed Theo.

'The FBI are hip to me. They're already close. I couldn't fly anywhere and besides I haven't a cent to my name.'

'It isn't looking perky. Why such exotic destinations?'

'The experience must cohere with the round world by containing tokens of the big scene. I have scraps from most places, but those three really sizzle and I got nothing.'

'Well, the round world is out of our reach. We are still hunted criminals and still penniless and that means immobility. Complete immobility,' concluded Theo. The plan was struggling under the weight of logistics – passports, money, the law, time, space and ethics – these loomed like freight trains over the hedgehog of their underground scheme. 'Lord help us,' sighed Spinny, inhaling on his ketamine-laced bifter, while Theo nodded in agreement, sipped his boysenberry and mango smoothie and nodded off.

While the philosopher took forty winks, Spinny stared out of his window. He needed to find a way of bypassing these obstacles to allow pan-continental liberty but his mind was foggy. Should he fail to succeed the project could go down the tube, down the sewer, to dust, to flowers, to reincarnations, to the mountain air, to dreams and visions only. He opened his treasure chest to avert depression and sniffed some Columbian marching powder, staring outside as his adrenaline started to romp.

Suddenly he saw a green flash that disappeared swiftly. Splash! Another two and then five tiny explosions of kryptonite pocked the near sky. Fireflies! He grabbed his binoculars and studied the insects and their luminous, yellow-green tinge; a spontaneous pin-prick of clarity against the mysterious cosmos. Once, while waiting for a bus, Spinny struck upon the idea that the speed of light changed[2]. He imagined light travelling faster at the moment of the Big Bang, and then as the universe cooled it slowed and stuck at its current velocity. If it is possible that light changed speed once, could it do so again?

'Theo!' he shouted, pouring a tub of freezing water over the

---

[2] Albert Einstein claimed that the speed of light, the c in $E=mc^2$, is as constant as the Northern Star and the steadiness of its velocity holds the universe in place, for reasons that are too complicated to go into here.

sleeping Englishman.

'Ai!'

'What if we change the speed of light? That will allow untraceable high-speed travel, and it won't cost a cent!'

'Sounds implausible,' Theo mused, wiping his eyes and drying himself with his jumper. The dubious hippie leapt up and began scribbling on his blackboard.

'Implausible? This is the best idea since Relativity!'

'You are going to have to explain what you are talking about.'

'Increasing the speed of light means bypassing the law and the state and bringing the planet into our back garden. It would allow us to outwit the restrictive laws of space and time!'

'I don't understand what that means. How can you speed up light?'

'If I push light beyond its regular velocity I can become untraceable.'

'How can you move light beyond its own speed?

'The metabolic whirring of fireflies produces their green glow. If you increase the vigour of its physiology with amphetamines, you could speed up the light that it produces.'

He rushed to the cupboard, pulled out a stash of amphetamines and captured the fireflies. Blessing each one, he promised they would be martyrs for the planetary cause and go to heaven, surrounded by an infinitude of whatever it is that fireflies are into. He soaked them in uppers while the tank heated and kinetic energy entered their bloodstreams so that both their organs and biochemistry became fast. This was amplified by his playing barn-techno which sent them into a frenzy of motion aggravated by the beaming of firefly pornography. Their bio-electric light intensified and blurred intangible like a wheel. After a short time in the microwave, Spinny blindfolded them and blared Hendrix so that all they had to go on was the psychedelic spin of their souls and the billowing guitars of 'All Along the Watchtower'. After a short pause, he opened the microwave and lay them on the desk. His beam-speed-orometer informed him that the fireflies were now emitting light waves at 600,000 miles an hour. Einstein, though undoubtedly a nice guy, was wrong.

chapter nine

The Rejection of Relativity

I

Spinny's first thought was for Theo to fire beams of light at his back and thus propel him to Africa, so he channelled them into a laser and told Theo to press the red button. He sat down comfortably with a motorcycle helmet and shouted 'Go!' but when Theo pressed the button the waves bounced straight off him. He then tried eating the light beams with some toast to speed up his own body, but they gave him nothing more than a mild tummy ache. He realised that he would need Calvin to develop a vehicle of some sort, perhaps with a transformer that could turn velocity into force.

'Now there are technical issues,' mused Spinny as he and Theo huddled around the blackboard in the lab. 'According to Relativity Theory matter cannot move at the speed of light. However, that is only true for the 4D universe. When you move light beyond its natural speed, you are promoted into 5D.'

'How?'

'This 4D universe of length, breadth, height and time rests on the foundation that light moves at a constant speed. If this speed changes the existence of the universe becomes incoherent. But the existence of the universe cannot be incoherent, so it has an in-built principle which immediately pushes head-fizzing problems up a dimension.'

'Hold up, there. What do you mean head-fizzing problems?' queried Theo.

'Some problems have the form of a mountain that must be conquered through sustained effort but others are of a different kind. They stump the mind, make you seasick with paradox and mystery so you cannot stand up straight. They are insoluble within our framework! Only by stepping outside of the box and forming a new framework can we piece together a solution. In the 19th century you had a theory of energy and a theory of matter and nobody could see how they fitted together until Einstein raised the bar. He introduced the curvature of space and the relativity of time and two distant cousins morphed into one being; $E=mc^2$.'

'Explain how this relates to your movement into 5D,' queried Theo.

'This shows how a head-fizzing problem can only be solved by thinking up a dimension. Making the speed of light faster than it is requires a new framework since our current 4D conception cannot cope with the idea.'

'Is this a scientifically acknowledged principle, this head fizzing stuff?'

'Kind of.'

'I have to say, Spinny, it sounds pretty whimsical,' said Theo.

'It ain't whimsical. This is what will allow me to convert the light waves into air pressure, bolt into the fifth dimension, twirl up space and then plop out over Africa.'

'What makes you think it will work?'

'The confidence and beauty of our souls will ensure success. Are you in?'

'Well, why stop here, eh? I mean it's not as if things are getting silly now,' Theo resigned, having given himself over to the bounce of Spinny's balloon. The alchemist returned to his desk and began to muse on how the vehicle would be fuelled, how it would reach critical mass without bursting into flames and how it could be steered safely at such high velocities and screech to a halt without turning the driver inside out with centrifugal force. Theo meanwhile had not quite left first base. His acceptance was passive, a note of surrender. His standing here in Ithaca with a lunatic alchemist attempting to change the speed of light was a cherry on the cake of the ridiculous. Even if the head-fizzing principle was true, it did not mean they could suddenly stroll through the fifth dimension. The possibility of flight was based on Spinny's belief that poetry, ecstasy and vibes – the subjective trinity of the soul – could create a scientifically functioning vehicle, rejecting the laws of logic. The thought was stupendous, and Theo realized that things had gone far enough. He simply had to regain control of his life and return to Cambridge. His criminal profile however was in some ways increasing while it decreased, since the longer he was missing for the more guilty he looked, but what could he do? He was being dragged behind the motorboat of Spinny's infectious ambition, waiting for the emancipating dolphin to burst from the waves.

Spinny locked himself away for several hours and Theo tried to get to sleep, but he was too wrapped up in anxiety and doubt. To his dismay, he was still awake in the small hours when Calvin's thumping, drunken steps came through the door. Listening closer, Theo could hear something else, quieter – the twitter of a skylark – yes! The soft timbre of the female voice! Theo jerked upright and pricked up his ears, and there was no mistaking it. Calvin had found a special someone.

They chatted and murmured, Calvin's voice transformed from its usual boom of curses and burps into mildness and manners. Suddenly, with a squeaky pop, the talking ceased. The Jimmy van Pokey was commencing, and the sounds of Calvin's porky body deflowering the poor waif filled the house.

At noon they heard footsteps tiptoeing to the front door and the soft click of release, and an hour later a serene Calvin descended the stairs. He swanned around in his cotton serong, often gesturing to the deep, passionate scratch marks across his back, but whether they resulted from an overflow of sexual ecstasy, or her desperate attempts to escape, we may never know.

Once his smugness had cooled to a bearable simmering, Spinny explained the idea. Calvin thought it was a hoot. After a short briefing he jumped in the van and headed down to North Carolina to collect parts. The boys waved him off and the technical phase of the project began.

'Airfternoon, fellas!' laughed Calvin, who had just arrived in Dayton, home of the Wright Brothers, speaking in a tone that was warm and formal.

'Mah name is Patrick Fineman, chief executive of the Western branch of the FCMJ national, state and federal department of media and foreign affairs in New York, spearheadin' the new project into data verification of early twentieth cennury all-American endeavours under Constitution Act 39, Section B. The amended version. Predicating the freedom of every man to build locomotory devices in the privacy of his own home. Our study is funded by the PLF, the Neter-National Railway association, Pan Am, British Airways, the FGTY, the YSUP, the SF and JPIOSJPKY, and a whole host of multinational corporations. It's to be reviewed in Congress in six months with a view to establishing once and for all the patent property of all ideas concerned with the dynamics of travel. Four and a half thousand law suits have been left unsuccessful or unresolved due to big ol' absence of any such study, and our project has attracted strong financial support from parsons as diverse as Shell, Woolworths, The Scientific American, New Scientist, Steven Spielberg and even goddamn Roger Pinkleman. I come here to this beautiful town of North Carolina to make an urgent request to photocopy the early designs of Wilbur and Orville Wright so as to figger whether the early materials used for the 'Kitty Hawk' glider were the idea of those all-American brothers. Some claim they come from Gustave Whitehead. There ain't no doubt in my mind that the idea was an American one, but should we fail to present evidence in the form of a photocopied design plan by the meeting next Fall, this Institute and Museum will be closed down and cease to receive funding. So, lemme photocopy the designs, and keep you in a job.'

The security guards were left reeling with all the numbers, figures and references in that torrent of nonsense and, impressed by the barrage of information, took him through to the archive room which was heavily protected with eye-laser detectors and fingerprint checkers. Calvin opened the trunk, took out the plans and looked through their designs. They were fairly simplistic compared to the F-15s and Stealth Bombers of today, but it was precisely in their simplicity that Calvin hoped to find the key. He stole all the parts relevant to him and gave the rest back. The two security guards looked puzzled at the depleted portfolio. 'I'll return them in a week,' Calvin reassured them. 'I knew you guys would understand.' On his way back to Ithaca he stopped off in various states to collect more engine and body parts from friends, relatives, work-pals and skips, and under instruction from Spinny he met a nuclear chemist in Ohio to collect some fissile materials. With all business done, he hurtled at a hundred and fifty miles an hour back to Ithaca, eyes popping with amyl nitrate and a ton of plutonium in the boot.

II

After surveying the blueprints of early biplanes, rockets and moon-buggies Calvin plunged into work. The appearance of nuts and bolts gave Theo a sense that Spinny and Calvin were going to construct this thing rather than just noodle around with goofy ideas. Seeing the instantiation of the idea in the form of lights and wings inspired Theo to stay on and have a peek. He had been a doubting Thomas for too long.

Spinny pointed out that before building the structure of the pod they had to know about how the fifth dimension worked. The only way to discover its operations was to study the superstring; a microscopic trestle of information telling us of the deep structure of the universe. The superstring would show whether five-dimensional space is crumpled or flat, extended or compressed. Problematically, to uncover a superstring requires temperatures of around 1032° Fahrenheit which Nils said the household oven was not equipped for, so Spinny rummaged around for any equipment that might help them. He managed to rustle together tubes, accelerators and the guitar amplifier on which Jimi Hendrix played 'The Star Spangled Banner' and spent twenty minutes rigging them up. Finally, he announced that the oven was ready.

Spinny took out a cube of ice from the freezer and put it inside. It melted, boiled and turned into steam. It soon seemed to have disappeared, but in fact the water molecules were rushing around more freely. Eventually, the energy of the individual water molecules exceeded the energy which bound them together, and they split into hydrogen and oxygen gases. The temperature in the oven was now getting pretty hot, and by the time it scaled 3,000° Fahrenheit, the hydrogen and oxygen atoms split apart, leaving an ionized gas. Spinny cranked up the amplifier to 1 billion degrees Fahrenheit, until the actual nuclei of the hydrogen and oxygen were separated, leaving nothing but neutrons and protons. Increasing the heat by another 10 trillion Fahrenheit, and with the neighbours starting to wonder what was going on, these neutrons and protons became quarks and leptons. At another quadrillion Fahrenheit an integration of electromagnetic and weak force took place, and at 1032° Fahrenheit, the symmetry of the superstring emerged. They paused while waiting for the dust to settle. Gingerly, Spinny approached the kitchen door and he opened it with his oven gloves to see that space-time had crunched and folded around itself. From behind him Theo could see in. It looked very similar in the kitchen to how the world looked when Theo was buzzing with liquid acid. In fact, the bent, crunched space-time continuum was the exact same.

Spinny pulled out the superstring, rushed it upstairs and peered at it under his electron microscope with the red and green 5D sunglasses which he had pocketed a few days earlier in the bottom of a cereal packet. He subjected it to various tests such as prodding, poking and squeezing and after two hours announced that space in the fifth dimension was unrippled, beige and roughly doughnut shaped. They retired for dinner in defiant mood, and since the oven was beyond repair voted for a Chinese. At Mao's they all shared wun-tun soup and crispy duck with pancakes. Drunk on Tiger beer and returning late, they decided to leave the kitchen until morning.

Calvin and Spinny locked themselves in the lab over the following week and experimented with various transformers. Eventually they found a way of converting velocity into force using condoms, orange peel and certain conductor metals. I am not going to go into the details of how they achieved this since it involves equations such as:

$$\frac{\epsilon\beta\upsilon\Pi*\iota\psi\varpi/}{\epsilon\delta\sigma4^{\tau}\eta^{\eta=}} = \Xi = \Xi\varphi o\epsilon 29\tau\eta$$
$$\delta\psi 2ov8\}\pi o\forall$$

Whilst this is an elegant and powerful theorem, explanation may alienate the lay reader and the only important thing is to know that it worked nice as a button.

Calvin took parts from the van down to the shed and attempted to construct the body, but numerous problems emerged. Having done some simple structural plans, Calvin realized that if the fifth dimension is doughnut-shaped then the vehicle had to be light to avoid sinking into the hole. He and Spinny calculated that the surface tension of the five-dimensional doughnut would buckle at fifteen stone. They worked this out using the Riemann metric tensor. The pod was going to weigh around six stone eight pounds, which left eight stone and four pounds for the traveller. Spinny, however, weighed eleven stone, and was planning for takeoff in a fortnight. At sixteen stone nine pounds, Calvin was out of the question, so they called Theo down to the shed.

'You may have to go,' said the alchemist severely.

'What?' cried Theo.

'I'm too heavy,' Spinny sighed. 'I can't lose three stone just like that. No way. I hardly eat a thing and I stay this weight. I'd have to cut off a limb and the pod can't get any lighter. Anything more than eight stone four pounds will sink it into the blue.'

'That's how much I weigh.'

'We thought so.'

'But this is your project, Spinny. I mean, this is your life's work!'

'Yeah but we're on borrowed time. Our neighbours know about us, the FBI is hot on our asses. I have a good feeling about you. You have drive. You are neurotic enough to look after yourself and you have a smooth, friendly face which will make it easier to get favours from foreigners.'

'I have to stop this madness. It's going from bad to worse. For God's sake I'm supposed to be doing my finals in a few weeks. What don't you ask Nils?'

'He won't make it. He'd probably spend his time meditating or teaching people how to find inner peace. I need someone with direction, someone restless who invites sympathy. Someone like you.'

'Well that is very kind, Spinny, but I don't think I can do it.'

'Theo, there's no choice!"

'No really, guys, it's not my thing. I don't have the constitution for it.'

'Break the line!'

'It's impractical. I mean, I have health problems, and I haven't got any money, or a passport.'

'That's why we got into all this in the first place, so it wouldn't matter.'

'Oh yes.'

'Theo, please! I'm desperate.' Theo could feel the pressure of their eyes and the longing in Spinny's brow. He saw humanity's religious poverty and an unstable global future. He saw his own middle-class sobriety. The trip seemed magical and dangerous, and Theo suddenly found himself mysteriously egged on once more by the pink flamingo of dissent. Acceptance would be far from easy. It meant a renunciation of certainty, a degree of sentimental trust, a career risk, a health hazard and a random pattern of circumstance (not to mention the small issue of his dissertation and his finals). Yet he felt again that his life as he knew it was over. That a truck had once again travelled across the universe with a second important metaphysical parcel, inside of which was the sensation that Theo must release his miserable grip of the river bank like a born-again crustacean and surf downstream on the babbling waters of Fate.

'You know what?' said Theo. 'I'll flipping do it!' Spinny grabbed his face and shook it, an expression of gratitude among alchemists.

'Now this is all groovy, but there is a problem with Theo,' Calvin said.

'What is it?' asked Spinny.

'The aerodynamic shape of the pod requires a sloped front windscreen slanting back at 70 degrees.'

'So?'

'Well I don't want to impinge on your, you know, as you say 'autonomy' at all, Theo, but, if you go you are going to have to get rid of that top hat. I know you never go anywhere without it, but you can't fit inside the cockpit with it.'

'My hat?' said Theo.

'Yes.'

'Sorry, guys. I have to draw the line there. I can't do that.'

'What?' exclaimed Spinny.

'I have worn it for eight years now, and it is the only thing that keeps my thoughts intact. Without it my life may descend into madness.'

'Are you calling all this sane?'

'True,' sighed Theo. 'It's just, well, after an eight-year relationship, I can't just leave it behind, you know. You guys don't understand.' As he uttered the words he realized his resistance was futile. The time had come to take decisive action against his neurosis and when you are flying at trans-dimensional speeds and becoming involved in world-saving activity, top hats can be very awkward. Theo sighed and, with an air of sadness, removed his top hat. Although it shredded his soul, he knew it was the only choice. The wind felt cool against his scalp. They congratulated him, and he felt strangely liberated. How open, how dynamic!

Night after night, Calvin was seen hammering fiercely, and Theo would look out from the smoky window feeling inspired after some mandolin practice and see the pod emerging. Spinny and Calvin spent hours standing beside the skeletal model with one arm folded and the other rubbing their chins. The house was getting more fetid, and the space-time in the kitchen remained warped. Recovering the superstrings had also buggered the oven, and they found no way to get a hot supper. For a while they warmed up their potatoes by taunting them. When that failed, Calvin suggested they use an indoor barbecue, and it worked pretty well although it charred the wallpaper quite badly and one night it set fire to the sofa and the Rhombus became a Square. Nils did become concerned about the house, but saw himself increasingly as an Engels figure, who by taking on the burden of his genius associates may be providing an invaluable service to the species.

During the construction process, it became clear that they would need something to stop the pod once it had reached the destination, and that no conventional break system would suffice. They required something that would exert massive influence without damaging the pod or its contents, some liquid force that could splatter with infinite power but not break the vehicle. They also needed to think about more trivial matters such as health and safety, for Spinny had made ominous predictions about the lift-off. The explosion would be loud and bright so they soundproofed the cockpit with old egg boxes, a trick that Theo had remembered from his days recording with the Renaissance quintet. To protect Theo's eyes from the scorching light, Spinny gave him a pair of Tom Robbins' sunglasses. For insulation during flight, they surrounded the outer cockpit with super-compressed titanium.

As pilot now, Theo occasionally voiced his concern over whether the thing would actually work. Spinny said the mechanics were scientifically sound but added that the nobility of their underlying ethos would charge it with life and flight. This was because the vehicle had arisen from the same intent as that of archaic man, who fashioned his muddy tools not to dominate the earth but to surf her rhythms. He struck up a symbiosis between the mosaic of inner experience with the awe-inspiring world of trees and stuff via primitive technology such as spades. Mechanistic technology such as the paper shredder, on the other hand, is inorganic and lacks the character of a hyperluminal pod crafted with warm feelings and naïve swells of hope. This pod, while being a flashy piece of quantum kit, also carried with it the mythical, unconscious and symbolic weight of man's deepest nature. The paper shredder lacks this mythic dimension.

Feeling slightly better about the chances of flight, Theo inquired about his job on the journey, and Spinny sat him down around the Square and began to explain his mission as Calvin attached the wheels.

'Any point on the earth is a fingerprint of that area. Its history, whether climatic, atmospheric, geological, industrial, cosmic – heck, even the pressure between crust plates – can be spotted in a leaf or pebble. I have collected a back catalogue but three spots remain. The first destination is Ghana. The scorching heats have thinned the soil, but Ghana is a fecund land. From here we need five grams of crushed cobra skin, two Henries of fresh jimson weed, a monkey tail and a splinter of sad wood.'

'What is a Henry?'

'Henry the eighth! An eighth of an ounce.'

'Ah.'

'The next destination.'

'Hang on. How am I supposed to steer to these places?'

'Don't worry about steering. The navigation system runs through a complicated magnet mechanism which draws the vehicle to certain lay lines where the forces of life hang heavy. Once you're in the fifth dimension the destinations can pull you in.'

'Okay. So what will the fifth dimension be like?'

'Fuck knows. You won't even notice. You will only be there for 0.001 of a millisecond.'

'Okay.'

'The second is Viti Levu, a tiny island near Papua New Guinea. It has a dense and lush rainforest overflowing with rare species, majesty and storms. Here you are to collect some palm honey, kava kava, a shot-glass of sea water and a whistling noise. And finally, from Spain, we need spray paint, the charred remains of a bohemian bonfire, milk of magnesia, the sole of an old man's sandal and a dash of female sexual fluid. The emotional intensity of the female sexual fluid will ensure that the compound is vibrant.'

'What do you mean female sexual fluid,' Theo asked.

'What?'

'Female sexual fluid. What on earth is that?' Spinny paused.

'How do you mean?'

'What is it?'

'You must know. I mean – don't you...'

'I've never been with a woman before,' announced Theo glumly, sinking into his chair.

'Oh Jesus,' said Spinny, throwing his hands up in despair. 'Never?'

'No. I wanted to tell you, but I felt embarrassed.'

'I can't believe you've never been with a woman before. I mean, what else have you been doing?'

'I've been focused on computer manuals.'

'Look Theo, I mean, are you gay?'

'No.'

'Ever done it with an animal?'

'No. Don't make a big thing, I just haven't had sex before.

Promise you won't tell Calvin?'

'Are you afraid of women?'

'No. God, I've tried hard enough. I really would like to – try it. I just haven't, well I've been so busy. I think I'm – the kind of person who would enjoy it. It's just not that easy these days.'

'Have you ever seen a vagina?' Spinny asked. Theo squirmed uncomfortably at the word. It made him tremble with fear yet a heady curiosity also.

'No. I mean... not in actual present reality. I've never been in the actual presence of an unclothed one, no. I've read about them though.'

'Well listen, Theo, you are going to have to get wise. I recommend practicing with some women along the way because, well you need to know what you are doing to get the fluid going, if you know what I mean.'

'Okay. I'll be alright. I'll just, you know, be confident. It's getting silly now, at twenty-one. It's time to – you know – do it. I'll get the fluid. I'm looking forward to seeing it, actually. It sounds fascinating. Can I keep some for myself?'

'You can do what you like with it,' said Spinny.

'Look at this guys,' said Calvin severely, laying the *Ithaca Times* on the table. A picture of Spinny and Theo lay on the front page along with a headline from the FBI asking if anyone had spotted them.

'Oh dear,' sighed Theo. Spinny was chastened. It was surely a matter of days before their capture, but they were too close to lift-off to relocate. All vehicles and properties were under surveillance and suspicion, and everyone in Ithaca was on their guard.

III

Calvin went into overdrive, labouring through the night on the photon satellite, the quantum laser and the tourbillon swerver while Spinny drove himself into sickness with the chemical transformers. The alchemist was often seen slumping in his chair looking depressed and concentrative, sporadically suffering ulcers, fever, inflammation and digestive bleeding; just some of the draw-backs of a renegade radio activist. However, leaps of imagination require strain, and finally Spinny cracked the break system. If left to ferment, boysenberry and mango smoothies often explode due to the build up of carbon dioxide. Spinny called upon Calvin to build a series of tailor-made smoothie bottles out of impervious platinum which suppresses the explosion until the pent-up energy reached nuclear levels. At that point the titanium cap blows off and the infinite energy of the smoothie is unleashed to stop the pod.

Once the bottles were ready Theo whipped up a cauldron of boysenberry and mango smoothie from Nils' Moorfield Organic Farm wages. Spinny collected fifty fireflies and laid them in beakers across his desk. He put them through the excitement process, and with the precision of an acupuncturist extracted their hyper-light with a tiny syringe. The light ran clear as the waters of a Tibetan stream and the first drop was pure... the spermatozoa of God!

By 9pm, the pod was complete. On a final safety check, Calvin tested its tensile strength and structural equilibrium by kicking it very hard and seeing if it broke. It did not break, and thus it was ready. He summoned everyone out to the shed, and they stood expectantly as he yanked the bed sheet away and revealed, in all her makeshift glory, *The Beagle Voyager*.

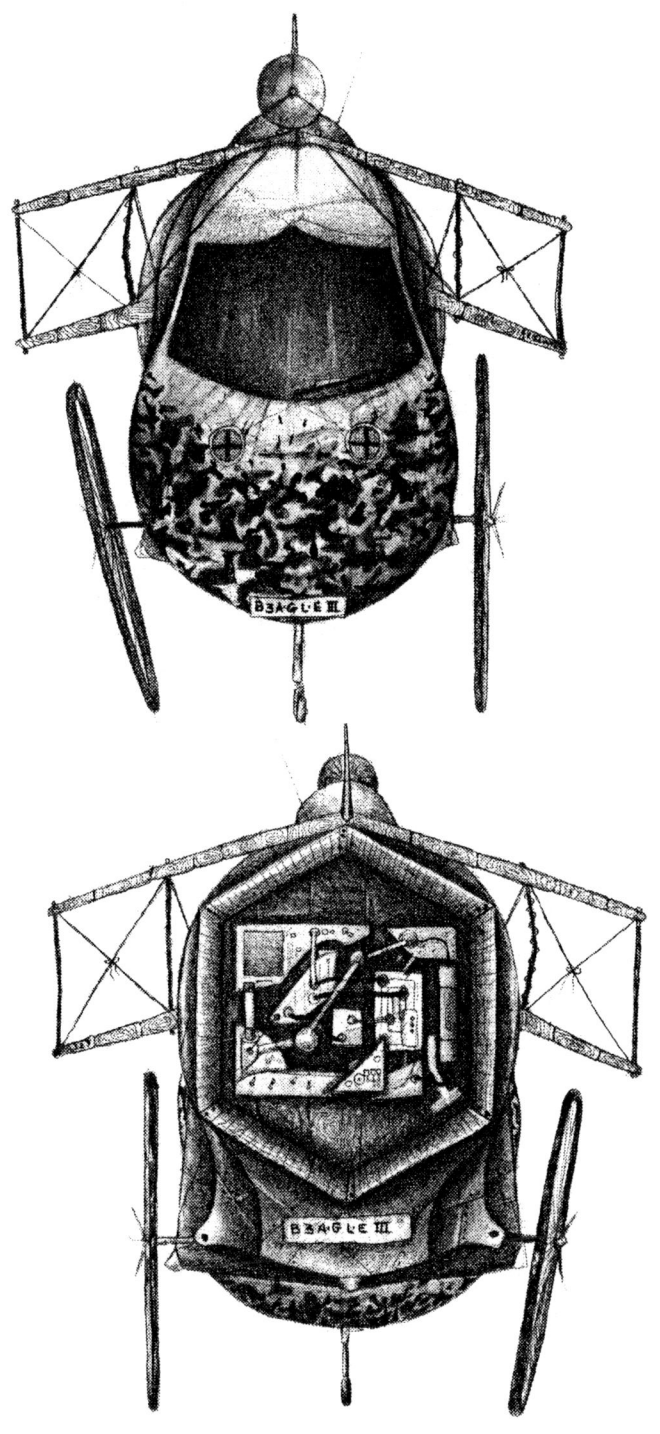

Lift-off would commence the next morning, and in celebration they threw a party. It was reckless considering their predicament, but they fell into whimsy. Calvin picked up pals and strangers from around the streets of Ithaca and they gathered in the garden with apple cider. It had been an intense ride and despite the tension and maddening mind-twist of it all the boys had been bound together by the glue of the work. Now that they were perched on the cusp of take-off there was a taste of glory somewhere between ginger and maple syrup. Despite his initial reservations, Theo was puffed up and did not fear the tigers and malaria of Africa, the pick pockets and venereal diseases of Hispanic peep-shows or the eerie mystery of this anonymous pacific isle. His future had gone from grey to orange and from orange to gold. Success would lift him to heroic heights for he would have saved human perception. Labia would quiver as women flocked to him like geese from every corner of the earth, especially Spain, and he would find himself perched at the throne of his generation surrounded by Cuban princesses, silk underpants and an infinite supply of mung beans, not to mention inexhaustible reading materials when he did find the time to get back to philosophy.

The visitors found the house pretty interesting but the place wasn't suited to a load of frivolous, drunken youths and it was only a matter of time before something went askew. One of the girls, drunk or stoned out of her wits, stumbled into the kitchen despite the large sign reading: 'DO NOT ENTER – SERIOUS SPACE-TIME REINTEGRATION IN OPERATION'. After one look inside, she ran around shrieking and flapping her arms in the way women do when they feel overwhelmed. If she expected reassuring words from the hosts, she would be disappointed. Spinny was drumming his fingers against things in a state of nervous tension while Calvin was more focused on putting drops of liquid helium into Nils' Echinacea tea than mollifying her panic. Not a great idea on Calvin's part. Nils had been talking to someone about the importance of listening and suddenly found his voice leaping up several octaves and breaking into fits of giggles. He remained unfazed, adapting the teaching to the importance of humour in the spiritual life but just as he was about to throw the floor open for questions, he started levitating.

'See!' he exclaimed as he rose ten foot above the ground, 'ze spirituality does work!' He reached fifteen foot, then twenty foot and then thirty, at which point he meditated on coming back down again.

'That'll teach you to dabble in Mongolian black magic!' shouted Calvin, but it was when Nils became a small speck that Calvin's mood changed. People gazed at the skyline as Calvin rushed to the FBI van and Theo followed suit. They zoomed down to the nearby airfield and hopped in a disused Spitfire Calvin used to work on and then flew over the house, scouring the horizon moving slow and high.

'What on earth is going on? Did he actually levitate?' queried Theo.

'Can you see him?' asked Calvin, as Theo stared through Spinny's binoculars.

'No. It's so dark. This is baffling.'

'Not really. I put liquid helium in his tea,' admitted Calvin.

'You did what?'

'I thought it would be funny.'

'You fool! You might have killed him.'

'Press the infrared button on the side,' said Calvin. 'We should be able to pick him up.' Theo did so, but the green screen showed no sign of Nils.

'I can't believe this. I can't believe we've lost Nils. What is going to happen to him? He won't last long up here. It can't be!' exclaimed Theo. They continued looking for three hours, but it was hopeless. They would never find him at that hour and by morning he would definitely be gone. They ran out of fuel but the airfield was closed so they had to land in a nearby field. For all his irritating, yoga claptrap, Nils was a good guy. He did not deserve to float into the atmosphere like that.

The next day was gloomy and Calvin was racked with guilt. He had always teased Nils because Calvin was blessed with a good deal of id. He was boisterous and fat enough to not be troubled by Nils' feverish need for meanings and patterns. For Calvin it was enough that life contained women, velocity, yeast and barbiturates. The thought of what lay beyond these things never entered the equation, for it tended to dull their edge.

That was why he put liquid helium in Nils' tea. It was to remind him of the absurdity of the human condition lest the hippie become too consumed with his own piecemeal spiritual development, to shake him awake and show that reality is muddy and we aren't heading anywhere special. A noble enough justification, but it had turned sour.

When Spinny learnt of how much helium Nils had drunk he took a sharp inhalation of breath, and anything that made Spinny take a sharp inhalation of breath had to be serious. He said that Nils would probably be shaving the edge of the stratosphere by now, and added that while they had gone searching for Nils there were rumours that the drunken girl had told the police about 12 Meadow View.

Calvin fuelled up the Spitfire for a daytime search the next morning and Spinny bundled Theo and *The Beagle* into a makeshift cooling chamber in the spare room to prepare them for the heat of the journey. There was an hour of solid stochastic cooling, during which Spinny tried to scramble all his things together. The house was in a terrible state, for although Nils had tried to keep it tidy and fresh he had been overcome by the forces of entropy. On the sideboard, two courgettes had formed a poisonous puddle, dripping onto a rock-hard slab of grey maggot-ridden pork. Dark yellow cottage cheese lay deceased and a furry carton of congealed milk was pissing on its grave. The avocados were wearing erudite glasses and translating *Das Kapital* into Mandarin. In the basement giant, fifty-foot tentacles moved like fat snakes, the entire room foggy with thick miasmatic gas of the most noxious ilk. It teemed with a billion ugly-faced seething insects buzzing like an ant-storm and a four-legged slimy alien was gyrating and salivating. Spinny shut the door, put a small ornamental table in front of it, and tried to forget about the whole thing.

Sirens were suddenly heard as the FBI vehicles glinted in the distance.

'Holy fuck!' shrieked Spinny. Theo burst out of the cooling chamber, preparing to flee the police as he recalled how all of this started all those light years ago. 'We have to move!' shouted Spinny meeting him on the stairs, and they gathered up the kit quick, lifted *The Beagle* and took it out to the garden. Spinny strapped Theo up, tying the elastic rope around his waist. Spinny shoved Theo's clothes in the clothes compartment, his maps and information in the maps and information compartment and his portable mandolin in the portable mandolin compartment as well as packing bits and bobs in a drawer under the driver's seat; compasses, pens, paper, a Swiss army knife and phrase books. He also stuffed some rugged army trousers under the dashboard which would stand Theo in better stead during the rough-and-tumble to come than his silken garments.

'Listen, Theo,' said Spinny. 'The firefly juice lasts one hundred days so you have to be home by the eighteenth of May. If you leave it any later you will either fail to lift off, or crash during flight. Now to be magnetically charged, the female sexual fluid has to be vibrating with emotional intensity on the 18th. The second it loses life, the whole mixture will disintegrate. She's got to be wild with excitement and I'm worried about your lack of sexual experience.'

'Is this really the time?' asked Theo.

'I want you to take this,' Spinny said, breathless, giving him a book on Taoist sex techniques. 'Make sure she's soaking with amour. If it's mechanical, it's dead. Don't fumble. Don't come too quickly. Don't act like a virgin and whatever you do don't fart. This book is full of tricks and techniques. You'll find some cool tips in there.'

'I'm not a square, you know.'

'Okay, Theo. Whatever you say,' grinned Spinny. All this attention and the oversized helmet made Theo feel like he was in Top Gun, a sensation aided no doubt by Highway To The Danger Zone which blasted mysteriously from giant cosmic hi-fi speakers in the clouds.

'Ready, champ?'

'Goddamn right, I'm ready!' yelled Theo and they embraced. 'Say goodbye to Calvin for me.'

'Sure will. Good luck out there.' Spinny closed the overhead screen and Theo lit the spark plug and the engine revved. The police smashed the back door, ran into the garden and told them to put their hands up but their demands were overcome by a thunderous roar as Calvin swooped fast and low in his Spitfire with a pumpkin dangling on a rope. Spinny jumped and flew off like a pink hero into the orange sun of Buddha. Moments later BOOM – *The Beagle Voyager* exploded in a billow of nuclear force towards the fifth dimension. Grass and flowers vaporized and the posts of the garden fence burst into flames like a hundred flicked matches. After the atomic blaze hung a wraith of smoky mystery, and a Doppler echo of Theo shouting 'Seize the day, motherfuckers!' as he went. So on that jubilant note, Spinny and Calvin fled to Mexico and Theo Fintwistle set off to collect the ingredients for human freedom armed with a woolly fleece, a flask full of broccoli soup and enough dried prunes to sink a small tanker.

END OF PART ONE

The Eternal Hut Boys
Ghana, West Africa

I

Theo was nervous about Africa. It is no place for a scholar. Let not his boisterous war-cry fool you, for when the Top Gun riff faded out he was left with a sense of disquiet. Some people say that it was from Africa that we all originated. Theo sided with the Lyellian theory that we came from the sea, and there were perfectly nice beaches in Norfolk. Sadly there was little time for cold feet now as the smoothie splattered over the pod and it screeched to a halt and squeezed back into three dimensions to drift over the red continent. He prodded his body, moved his limbs and blinked his eyes in disbelief. *The Beagle* was at an altitude of 15,000 feet which was slightly high but the radiator maintained an even temperature and the compression equaliser kept the air kosher.

An hour later he touched down in the market place of Accra, capital of Ghana. As the canopy swung open he felt the sun blare mega-heat upon black skin amidst streets awash with disease and the sick smell of boiling milk. Curious bony dogs whimpered in open sewers, broken cars farted noxious exhaust fumes and the smell of frying plantain was giddying. 'Brawfonyo!' shouted stunned children at the mysterious white man who appeared out of nowhere. Market sellers mauled him, gleeful boys leapt onto *The Beagle* and Theo tried to shoo them away with his walking stick, wrestling through the crowds to find some space to gather himself. Hassled and hounded, he finally reached an outhouse on the periphery and took out the map and instructions Spinny had written for him. He approached a non-hysterical old man and asked for directions. The old man looked at the paper with infinite dark eyes and pointed Theo towards a dirt track that ran along the distant beach. Leaving the heaving masses behind, Theo dragged the heavy pod through the dust and debris. It took an hour to reach the beach and Theo kept choking on the sandy wind, his translucent skin sizzling like egg-white in the equatorial glare. 'Blimey,' he muttered, 'this is lunacy! What the hell am I doing?' He had spared little thought for the magnitude of this expedition and the task that now confronted him.

He followed the dirt track and the handwritten signposts to Mamprobi and arrived hours later in the Chet Baker of nightfall. Inky blackness hung over the adobe huts and the slow-burning lamps shed glimmers of light over the shanty settlements. Men spoke intently under flickering streetlights and the atmosphere was thick with their words while grandfathers sat on crates with their legs crossed and watched the shooshing Atlantic wash its foamy surf onto the shitty beach.

Theo approached a group of fishermen and asked if they knew 'Chaplain'. They looked at Theo and shook their heads and he moved on to ask several other men. His fifth inquiry was met with a nod and he was directed towards a large and complex hut perched on a sanddune overlooking a dilapidated pier. As the philosopher neared he saw two figures sat on a porch beneath the choppy shine of a faulty lightbulb, enshrouded in a plume of smoke and studying a book. Their chanted prayers were hypnotic in rhythm and rumbacity. Not wanting to disturb them, Theo parked up *The Beagle* and changed into some clean clothes. When the prayer ceased a chalice of weed was lit and a lighter mood ensued, so Theo advanced through the bushes and approached them.

'Rastafari!' came the salute from Chaplain as the pale philosopher emerged from the darkness.

'Hello there,' said Theo.

'My Lord, what be ya name?'

'Theo Fintwistle. How do you do? I am a friend of Spinny.'

'Ah!'

'Munbago?' asked Tataguan (pronounced tata-gwan), the taller of the pair.

'Kashik! How is Spinny! Blessings rain on him.'

'He sends his regards to you too.'

'My Lord, what is that?' asked Tataguan, gesturing to *The Beagle* behind him.

'Oh it's my pod. It's nothing really.'

'Grand Duke Fintwisty!' shouted Tataguan.

'Oh no,' said Theo. 'I'm not a Grand Duke. I write computer manuals.'

'I bow to each man,' Tataguan went on, kneeling before Theo and kissing his toes.

'Erm, I wouldn't do that if I were you – they are pretty stinky.'

'My Lord, thank you. Sweet feet!' he said, getting up and returning to his seat.

'Bush?' Chaplain asked, offering the chalice to Theo.

'Golly,' he sighed, removing his smoking jacket. 'Don't mind if I do!' Theo took a toke and felt the smooth creamy flow elevating his soul as the tangled fishing net of his mind unwound and the soul-lamp burned. Sitting on a spare chair, he looked around the hut.

The Jerusalem classroom was a hand-built home split into four sections. Chaplain's room was enclosed and joined to the porch while a wooden beam curbed around the bench and led towards Tataguan's smaller room. In the other section lived 'Garvey'. He always read Marcus Garvey and was known as Garvey. In the front porch was one chair with two smaller ones squashed together to form a bench next to a faded table scratched and dented, leaning on rickety legs. Cuttings of weed accumulated in the dents and scratches and during droughts Chaplain would fish them out with a twig.

'Eh, Teo. You must be tired?' asked Chaplain seeing his red eyes and sagging shoulders.

'Yes, I am a bit,' sighed Theo as the weed calmed his agitated energy.

'Take sleep sure!' said Chaplain, who went into his room and pulled his sponge mattress off the bed and lay it down on the sand by the side wall.

'Oh, thank you,' said Theo. 'But before I sleep I need to talk to you about why I am here.'

'Shh,' smiled Chaplain. 'Take rest. We speak tomorrow.'

'Yes, okay. We'll speak tomorrow. No hurry is there!' and Theo lay down, took off his sandals and within eight seconds was fast asleep while the Rastafarians sat in silence and occasionally said something about God.

In the morning Chaplain and Tataguan were nowhere to be seen. Theo washed in the sea, combed his hair and after checking that *The Beagle* was okay set off on a walk around the area. An old fat woman with soft arms swept her hut with a broom of corn ears and the dust was buzzing with the prattle of dirty infants. *Fufu* was pounded in wooden bowls and the dark red juices of soup sprayed onto the sand to be slurped by deformed, clucking chickens. Children ran after Theo and offered him nuts, banana skins and pieces of torn cloth. Congregating around him, they would hold hands, stroke his leg and stare. He moved on to inspect the crumbling roads, soft-drink stalls and strutting mothers fat and powerful. At midday he returned to the Jerusalem classroom to speak to Chaplain and get the project going.

'Eh, we thought you leave!' exclaimed Tataguan as Theo ambled through the bushes. 'Time for food, irie?' he said, pointing to the assortment of dishes laid out on the damaged table.

'Great,' said Theo, taking his place. 'Sorry about that. My, what a place this is!'

'Dis is Garvey,' said Chaplain, and Theo shook hands with the slightly podgier member of the crew. 'Now eat!'

Theo tucked into his *fufu*, a round beige stodge in a bowl of red soup. It was consistent and speckled with dark freckles, salty and chewy. The spicy soup burned the roof of Theo's mild mouth and forced him to drink a pint of sewer water as the doughy mass worked its way down his throat. His stomach made odd noises as it tried to figure out what to do with the stuff since it had been a long time since even his ancestors had eaten *fufu* (after the long trek north the western body had adapted to things like crisps and jam). In the middle of the table was a bowl of long corn sticks that looked like curly pencils. They were crunchy as pretzels with a maizy taste that was bread-crummy at first and then sweet.

After meals Chaplain always played a fugue of thanks to God on his banged-up guitar with four strings missing, followed by a few minutes of noodling around. Noticing that Theo was watching his finger technique, Chaplain asked if he played the guitar. Theo said he played the mandolin and Chaplain asked for a rendition. As a bedroom mandolinist Theo was not easily given to public performances, and he had hardly played in recent weeks, but Chaplain's twanging inspired him so he took his instrument from *The Beagle* and tuned up. He played them 'Ride of the Valkyries' and there was a weighty silence.

'Bootiful!' whispered Chaplain.

'Oh, thank you.'

'Let us play together, guitar and mandolin!'

'You mean... have a jam?'

'Ya. Jammin.' Theo had never jammed before but felt having fled the FBI, taken seven cubes of liquid acid and travelled at 600,000 mph in the fifth dimension it was about time he pushed the boat out and tried to play a bit of unscripted music. He twirled a riff and Chaplain dropped some quirky chords. A groove settled and Chaplain tapped his foot and sang 'Dobaday' on the three of each four. As Theo's confidence grew he did a gratuitous solo and Chaplain moved into the sad breakdown. They played all afternoon and deep into the night, the skin of Theo's fingertips worn away and his place on earth justified.

'Eh, Teo,' said Chaplain as the session wound down, Tataguan and Garvey fast asleep. 'Dere is no limit. People study moosic theory – to know right in da note, da right scale- Gwan! I bought some book, got deep and keep failing and see. I tell the truth I know dese chords. Moses was a clean man. Him no school but just empty in Jah flow, you nar?'

'I think so,' said Theo. Chaplain grinned, lay his guitar down and headed for bed.

'Er, Chaplain, I need to speak to you about this project.'

'Tomorrow,' smiled Chaplain. 'Tomorrow.'

Inspired, awake, and a little tense about his failure to get the project started, Theo had difficulty sleeping so he leafed through Tataguan's Bible. Instead of sending him to forty winks, the faded pages exercised gravity on the philosopher. The parchment made the world heavy and substantial, and was laden with the anguish of centuries. By the time he passed Deuteronomy he was primed to meet his maker and headed down to the seafront to sleep with the stars as his roof, identifying that empty darkness with the Almighty.

By dawn Theo had been ravaged by mosquito bites, tossing and turning with the mad ecstasy of tropical itches. When he gave in and scratched the itch it returned with an army of brothers. He stabbed himself with his emergency pencil to focus on a sharp point instead of a dull mist but when the tip of his pencil finally became blunt, he gave up and walked back to the Jerusalem classroom. Chaplain and Tataguan were nowhere to be seen again that morning – perhaps they worked mornings? – but a skinny chap named Johnson sat by their table packing a pipe. He often sat alone and smoked in the faded day, his small and indestructible body draped in ragged clothes. Johnson was friends with the vicars but lived on a philosophy of hard taekwondo training and self-discipline, whereas they lived a pretty bum life of smoking vast amounts of weed and dozing. Johnson smoked occasionally, but only to mellow the pressing discomfort of his environment.

'Eh! Chaleh[3]' exclaimed Johnson with a bounce. When he spoke he leant up close to Theo and his laughing ears almost met at the back of his head.

---

[3] pal, chum or friend.

'Hello. I'm Theo.'
'Johnson. It is nice to see someone as you here.'
'Oh thanks. Yes, I am just here for a little while.'
'Dat is best. If you can come and go dat is good for you. No need to stay,' he laughed.
'Oh, I don't know. I rather like it here.'
'Ah! Chaleh, how long you in Ghana?'
'A few days now.'
'So after FEW DAYS! What a beautiful place you say but stay for year, two year den see slowly dat in Ghana here dere is not much. We are stuck. It is like dis. People from white places a come and say 'ah, away from rat race!' So you call it? But if you stay too long you miss comfort and adrenaline.' He smiled. 'But you are here now, so I tink da important ting is for you to come to know us and dis place so you can understand it and maybe remember. To tell people about Ghana here and to know how it is.'
'Yes I would like that. I mean, I have quite a lot of work to do, but I am hoping to see some sights. Are there museums around?'
'No. I want you to see Ghana and know how it is not in museum no. Look, where are you from?'
'England.'
'Da Land of Phil Collins!' Johnson laughed.
'Sorry?'
'I can feel it coming in de air tonight... oh jah! What a song. In Ghana here we love da Phil Collins. What do you do dere?'
'I study and write computer manuals.'
'Ah! Tings of the mind,' he said, leaning forward and pressing his index finger against his temple. 'In white country you can be lucky and go to library. I was student – politics at Kumasi. Now I see something too and affer I tink about God. You see when ah put God to question I profess not to know da first cause BUT if man can find explanation widout resorting to miracles he should.'
'Yes.'
'You are not strong, Teo.'
'Sorry?'
'You are clever but not strong. You see,' – and he poked

Theo in his soft belly – 'Come, let us kick pumpkin.'

'Pumpkin?'

'Yes. Follow me.'

'Eh, I can't really. I have to wait for Chaplain to return to speak to him. I have to get my work underway.'

'Eh, Chaplain and Tataguan fetching weed today. Not back till affer.'

'Oh.'

'Come we make strong.'

'Well okay, why not,' sighed Theo, who was starting to suspect that his work in Ghana would not be quick. Johnson led him up the beach and they came to a cleared spot where a dishevelled pumpkin dangled at the end of a rope tied to a climbing frame.

'Fool do press up for strength, but strength come from thighs and belly. Your belly is weak, like everyone from land of Phil Collins but thigh also weak becar you do not HIKE. I want to make thigh strong so if you attacked by bandits you can lick dem wit fire.'

'I can do what?'

'Lick dem wit fire. O sorry! Chaleh it's an expression. Tataguan always shout at Pope man becar Pope say man get to God tru him. Yet Tataguan feel man get to God direct so when Pope say tru him Tataguan say 'Lick fire 'pon Pope – kick da Pope, let lion on da Pope and his Pope Waze, see?'

'I see.'

'So if you attacked you lick dem wit fire.'

'Right-o.'

'Stand here,' he commanded. 'Kick pumpkin!'

'What just kick it?'

'Just tap it with foot. Hold leg in air and tap.' When Theo tried to suspend his leg in a kicking action his thighs trembled with weakness. 'See!' said Johnson, tapping his temple with his index finger. 'Da mind okay, but da body...O!' Theo struggled for half an hour to hold his leg up and kick the pumpkin slowly and was relieved when Johnson announced the session was over. He then took out a small red and white book from his bag and said, 'Repeat affer me!' handing Theo a pencil. Theo sat on a rock feeling bemused and Johnson paced around, compelled by the idea of turning him into a taekwondo warrior.

'HAIL SELASSIE! The Lord of Strength! Give me power in morning and afternoon and make sure I eat *kenke* and *fufu*. Got it?'

'Yes, hang on a second, yes.'

'I resolve to train hard to walk upright tru valley. Okay?'

'Yes. Do go on.'

'Valley of darkness. Make dat valley of darkness.'

'Okay.'

'Dis is diet. Water in morning. Groundnuts. Five hours of training. Den *kenke* den six hours den *fufu* den stretching den sleep. You do dis for two year and you be okay.'

'Two years!' Theo exclaimed.

'Yes, two year.'

'Oh no, I really can't train for two years.'

'One year den,' said Johnson looking up.

'No, I can't train for one year either.'

'What, are you trying to fuck me?'

'No I'm not. I just... I have things to do. I can't just take a year off. I was hoping to go for a jog occasionally.'

'You tink it come so easy?' asked Johnson sucking his teeth, 'tsk.'

'Oh let's just forget it shall we?'

'You are not copying dis down are you?'

'Of course not.' Johnson looked at his watch and tutted. 'Come, we must get you some food. You are tired dat is why you not keen to stay for two years,' and he gathered their things and they headed back to the Jerusalem classroom.

'How long can you train for?' he asked as they walked.

'A couple of weeks maybe.'

'COUPLE OF WEEKS! Ach, what do you tink can be done in couple of weeks?'

'Look it was your idea.'

'You can do nothing in a couple of weeks.'

'So let's not bother.' The sweat from the training was crystallising and as they walked Theo felt agitated and kept scratching, which bought the mosquito bites back to life. They walked in silence, following the scent of the vicars breaking into a new batch.

'Mosquitoes are bloody awful out here,' said Theo, trying to change the mood.

'Ah. You be careful.'

'Too late for that. Last night they turned me into Ulysses in brail.'

'You get the bite... den malaria!' Johnson warned sternly.

'Malaria?'

'Yes, very bad. Headache, hot, cold. Not irie.'

'Is it fatal?'

'For me no. But for you maybe. You not strong enough for malaria. Be vigilant!'

'Eh Johnson,' shouted Chaplain as they returned to the hut. 'You meet da chaleh!' and they tapped fists.

'Teo how? You sleep on beach?' asked Tataguan.

'Yes,' said Theo.

'You learning taekwondo. Ha-yah!' Chaplain screamed in a mock-Chinese accent and hit the table with his fist. 'Punch me buttocks Teo!' he said, pointing his tense buttock towards the furrowed philosopher.

'Listen Chaplain, I need to speak to you about this project. I need help.'

'Punch me buttocks!' Chaplain shouted again.

'Oh for God's sake,' sighed Theo, launching a half-hearted punch on his rock hard buttocks.

'Okay, now we speak,' Chaplain said, loading his pipe and sitting back down. Theo was relieved to finally get the ball rolling.

'Right. Now me and Spinny—'

'Ah Spinny? How is he?'

'He's fine. Now me and Spinny—'

'Spinny and I, Teo! Where da English?' asked Johnson, throwing a stone up and catching it for leisure.

'Spinny and I are in a project and... I need to gather some materials from here to take back to America.'

'To where my Lord?' asked Chaplain.

'America.'

'BABYLON!' shouted Chaplain standing upright and punching his fist into the air.

'No, America.'

'Da Satan!' mirrored Tataguan.

'What are you talking about?' asked Theo. Chaplain looked severe.

'Dem America bring world down. Wit dey cosmetics and consumption.'

'Consumption!' repeated Tataguan.

'You have no place dere. Neither does Spinny. I telling him to stay in Ghana here,' he announced and sat back down again.

'Well look, America has got problems but that is exactly why we are involved in this project.'

'America and West bring down!' Chaplain shouted standing up again. 'Dey need to curb deir obsessions.'

'Obsessions!' shouted Tataguan.

'Thwart the world. I want no involve with dat place. You not take anything from Ghana here to dat place,' and he sat back down.

'But you see—'

'Like Rome, Teo, when she fall like meteor whole world fall. Too big! Chaleh, man should live in beach-hut, stable. I no job, no car, no swimming pool. Atlantic in dem mah swimming pool. Who has swimming pool to compare?'

'The Atlantic isn't your swimming pool.'

'It is! Ask anyone,' Chaplain boasted.

'Excuse me!' Theo called out to someone in a neighbouring hut. 'Who owns the Atlantic?'

'Chaplain,' he said.

'See!'

'This is stupid,' sighed Theo.

'Different views interact!' said Johnson, who always sat quietly during arguments and occasionally made very general observations.

'All day I lounge in me chair and pray and smoke,' Chaplain went on. 'We rustle up food and be good. Jah provide!'

'Who?'

'Jah.'

'Who is that?'

'Jah Providence, Jah is da free breeze. The world come in and go, who else but Jah?'

'What is he, a friend of yours?'

'Me best friend!'
'Sounds like quite a guy.'
'Aye, misunderstanding...' mused Johnson.
'Grow ya dreadlocks and stay in Ghana. Do not go to America,' Chaplain concluded.
'It isn't just America. England is as bad you know.'
'Nah! England wise. Refined.'
'I'm not sure about that.'
'But England land of Phil Collins!' exclaimed Johnson.
'Yes, Phil Collins was born in England but I don't see what that has got to do with it.'
'Don't go to dat America,' Chaplain said firmly. The pipe was passed around and everyone morphed into the mist. Theo felt irked and concerned that Chaplain was refusing to help. Until he could find someone to lead him towards monkeys, cobras and bancha twigs Theo was impotent and he had expected assistance, so he opened up *The Beagle* to see if Spinny had left any advice about what to do if the project was constipated. Spinny had indeed written in the notebook, 'If things are slow or bunged up, practise sex techniques!' Theo consoled himself of his difficulties by realising that he could at least start learning those until the wheels started turning. He opened the draw under the dashboard and waded through the papers and maps, finding the purple book and heading down to the beach to begin reading.

Leafing through the early pages it was clear that the Taoist approach to sex was quite different to Theo's scholarly, Catholic-Calvinist, Anglo-Saxon negative vitality. Back in his Cambridge days he had always imagined sex as a kind of ordeal. The whole rigmarole of combing your hair, applying aftershave and entering an overpriced disco without being turned away by mean bouncers was only the first stage. One must then dance without looking like a nincompoop, avoid getting beaten up, scour for a mate, secure a mate and find an appropriate bedroom. As if this wasn't hassle enough, one must endeavour to undo the brassière quickly, remove your underpants sexily without getting your legs wrapped around each other, excite the female, press the right bits, don't cramp, be rhythmic without being mechanical, supply her with at least one orgasm and then, finally, take the act to its logical, expansive conclusion. It was a feat of engineering more than a flirt with divinity.

For the Taoists sex was a mystical act where humans participate in the fundamental energies of the universe, and the longer one participates in the fundamental energies of the universe the better, they felt (and who could blame them?) In concrete terms this meant longer, better love-making through hard training in which one learns how to engage in multiple positions, spread the energies throughout the body and raise the magnetism of attraction to well nigh explosive levels until the two souls dilate into one harmonious 'roger me!' Whilst the logician in Theo scoffed, the idea of day-long sex and multiple orgasms was too intriguing to be sniffed at and provided a welcome escape from the stuttering failure of the project and the stuttering failure of his own sex life.

The first practice involved breathing in, lifting the testicles up and imagining the cool 'chi' energy rising up the back and touching the pa-hui at the crown of the head and then, pressing the tongue against the roof of the mouth, allowing it to fall down into the belly. Chi travelled along the 'microcosmic orbit' – a kind of internal big-dipper – and as it went it handed out flags and party-poppers to the meridians on the way. It was a bit of quick thinking on Spinny's part. The end of this project would be sexual union, a union in which Theo had precious little experience (none, in fact). The emancipation of the species would depend on his performance, which is quite a burden. However these practises and tips would stand him in good stead, and they weren't limited to the act alone. There were many extraneous tips concerned with exercise and diet including a recommendation to eat walnuts to increase sperm production. He began the testicle breathing and sure enough felt a tingling in his pa-hui and his meridians generally perked up leaving him sitting in a dizzy and contented trance.

'Teo – are you angry?' asked Johnson, kicking sand and scuffling up behind Theo while the vicars talked about God.

'No no,' Theo said. 'I just wanted to look at this book. It's very interesting you know.' Johnson picked it up and frowned.

'Taoist Sex. Eh, Teo, are deir pictures?'
'Not sure.'
'Ah well. Teo I want to speak with you.'
'Yes?'
'In dis project – ah can help you. I want to help you because I tink you are my friend.'
'Really?'
'Yes. What do you need?' Theo stood up and had a little head rush and, after steadying himself, went to *The Beagle* and took out the list.

'That would be great, if you could help. There are a few things here. A cobra skin, a monkey tail, jimson weed and a splinter of sad wood. And a bancha twig. I can get a splinter of sad wood from anywhere, and jimson weed from Chaplain perhaps if I don't say anything. It's the cobra skin and monkey tail that are problematic.'

'No. Chaplain weed is not jimson. It is gem. For jimson you go to Kumasi.'

'Oh right.'
'Cobra skin... I think yes. We can find it at Kakum.'
'Where?'
'National Park. In Northern region – we alwaze go! Come tomorrow – we rise with da sun and hobble on tro. I can see you are keen to start.'

'Okay.'
'I come for you at dawn?'
'Eh, can we leave later in the morning?'
'No Teo – dawn.'
'Okay.'
'Good. I excited. Now listen, go to Chaplain and say sorry. Make up for argument so no low feelings.'

'Yes.' Johnson put his clenched fist out, and Theo clenched his and tapped it. He put the Taoist book and list back in *The Beagle* and followed the sounds of Chaplain's guitar.

'Hi Chaplain. Let's forget about, you know, what we were talking about.'

'Of course!' Chaplain laughed. 'More important is friendship and music, so listen. I want us to make friends and write a tune. A tune I have written but I tink we can collaborate. It go like this,

'I wrote thousands of letters
you did not return them to me.
Promise to come back.
When are you coming home?
How long you gonna live in a strange land?
I wish I'm away
'cos I say yay!'

'What do you think?'

'I love it,' said Theo, whipping out his mandolin. 'What are the chords?'

'A minor, den G and den C.'

'Let's play.' They spent the next four hours on the tune, Theo helping Chaplain with a few lyrical tips (such as informing him that 'yay' is not a word). He dropped in some diminished fifths, a new double-time bridge and two contrapuntal harmony lines reminiscent of a baroque fugue. Losing track of time, they were lost in the buzz of creative discovery, became friends again and fell asleep at four.

II

Johnson poked Theo in the cheek the next morning and Theo gradually roused to see a thoughtful face grinning at him.

'Oh pants,' sighed Theo. 'I'm so sorry!' and he jumped up and gathered his things.

'No problems. But we must head now to get to northern region in time,' said Johnson seriously.

'Sure, sure. Let me just pack my toothbrush and some spare clothes. Do we need any food for the trip?'

'Jah provide!' said Johnson.

'Oh is Jah going to be there? Wonderful. I can't wait to meet him.'

'Come, come.' Theo zipped up his rucksack and they set off. As they approached Accra, Theo noticed that Johnson was holding his head up, puffing his chest and clenching his jaw.

This was common for Rastafarians and people of pantheist persuasion. Any urban development was a manifestation of Babylon – a sprawling oppressive power complex – and thus an enemy to their Abraham ideal. The pace and temper of third world cities was the antithesis of stoned beach-religion. Although Johnson did not subscribe to the full blown laziness of his horizontal buddies, he held to the principles of a simple, contemplative life in nature and was opposed to the smoggy, fume-filled hothouse of Accra.

The tro-tro[4] station was heaving, thousands of muffin sellers swarming like flies around the windows of each bus. In the push and shove, Theo and Johnson were separated and two men shoved Theo to the floor and took his wallet and pocket-watch. Johnson heard Theo's yelp and turned around. When he found the helpless Englishman on the floor he flew into a rage, running wildly around the place looking for the thieves but it was no use. Theo got up, dusted the sand from his cotton waistcoat and told Johnson to calm down.

'Da Babylon fuck! Dis what Chaplain say. Man not right in city,' Johnson flamed.

'Okay, okay, let's settle down now. I wasn't hurt and I have more money hidden in my shoe.'

'Shoe?'

'I always keep money hidden in my shoe in case I get mugged.'

'Still. Dey make saga. BAM dey lick you. You should kick dem like pumpkin.'

'It was all so fast and besides, my taekwondo skills are not at practicable levels just yet.'

'Fuck!'

'Just take it easy – why are you going so mad?'

'I angry,' he sighed. 'Becar I want you to see Ghana here. I want to show you my country becar we are friends and I want

---

[4] Tro-tros are banged up minibuses with no tyres and coat hangers for gear sticks. Small planks of wood replace the snapped accelerators but somehow they seem to splutter and jerk to their destinations most of the time.

to help you and I do not want you to see dese things. Dey are dere.'

'Well let's just get the bus and get out of here before we get mugged again, eh?'

'Yes.' They boarded the Kakum tro-tro; a most forlorn vehicle with no windows, one wheel missing and a sticker on the back saying 'Prince of Peace and Motion'. Soon after taking their places at the back a preacher boarded and began to lead singing. His role was to pacify the passengers' souls in case this was to be their last journey.

Africa rushed past them. The black and chaotic fog of Accra dispersed and the unbroken rooftops became bitty settlements peppering the barren land. Theo munched on some corn sticks he had bought just in case Jah wasn't around at the other end, and Johnson stared concentratedly out of the missing window.

'Da world is boring,' he announced.

'How so?' asked Theo, enjoying the cool air rushing in through the hole in the roof.

'It is unusual.'

'That is not the same thing.'

'Oh but it is, Teo. Think of a cup of water. If I get cup of water every morning it is boring. But if one morning I get a cup of orange juice, it is unusual but STILL boring, eh?' Johnson laughed, his sense of profundity taking his mind off the mugging and putting it back on his ongoing attempt to grasp the universe with an obscurely brilliant thought. Theo leant back and after a couple of rounds of testicle breathing mused on the project. He felt that after a slow start he was now tuning in to the synchronicity that would lead him to the treasure, and Johnson would be his guide.

As the sun clocked out and the moon checked in, the tro-tro somehow arrived in the Kakum and the last passengers gathered their bags and left. Theo followed Johnson towards a parade of outhouses. It was too late to hike to the Kakum so they would rest for the night and set off early, Johnson finding them a room and Theo paying with his emergency cash from Calvin's profits. The lady offered them food and Johnson nodded so she sat them down at a table beneath an open wooden frame as a television burned in the corner. An hour later she arrived with two plates of green chicken and rice. Johnson ate the whole chicken and the bone to keep his colon mighty, and Theo had a couple of bites and drank several glasses of water.

'Okay? We sleep,' said Johnson, gathering their plates and taking them to the kitchens. Theo trudged wearily to the room and lay their bags down. It was adorned with mosquito nets, a wooden floor and two simple beds. Johnson came up some minutes later and did an hour of sit-ups and kicking practise but Theo declined the invitation to join him in preference for rubbing his cheek against the pillow. Theo was soon asleep while Johnson sweated, muttered a little to himself about truth and slept also.

At dawn Johnson leapt up and packed their things and Theo blinked his eyes and arose and the two of them set off while the sun was cool. They hiked towards the Kakum over hilly and jaunty land and although Theo was hungry the exercise enlivened him. When they reached the National Park Johnson spoke to a friend of his at the entrance turnstile who listened carefully and advised them to head to a monkey sanctuary where a man called Winston would help them. Johnson and his friend tapped fists and the boys headed around the Park and reached the marshy lake which surrounded the monkey sanctuary.

The sun grew fierce during their wait for action, and it was not until deep into the afternoon that Winston finally emerged across the river. He had powerful, deep-set features with thick scars across both cheeks. Johnson spoke to him in Twi, a local dialect, and he nodded and stared downwards and when Johnson finished speaking Winston looked at Theo for a moment and then turned around and unmoored a wooden canoe that lay strapped to the bank and ushered them in. Johnson and Theo stepped inside and with a light push off they cut through the unbroken waters. Sinking low, Theo trailed his fingers along the surface of the lake leaving small eddies and whirlpools of disturbance.

Johnson was deep in thought and did not notice some minutes later when they passed a goat on fire. It was being burnt alive on a crucifix. Around it there was an exotic ceremony; eight men thwacking their drums and women dancing with their eyes rolling back in their heads in some bio-mystical release.

'Blimey O'Reilly! Why is there a burning goat there?' exclaimed Theo. Johnson said nothing but sat with his head down concentrating. 'Johnson! Why is there a burning goat there?' Johnson looked up and saw the crackling, blackened creature with its horns nailed up.

'It's nothing.'

'What do you mean nothing?'

'Dey just burn da goat occasionally. Ritual,' and he put his head down again.

'A religious ritual?'

'Yes. At certain time when something happen dey celebrate with da burning goat.'

'Horrendous! They just buy them or something?'

'No, just take dem. Goat be everywhere. Pick one up and lick with fire. He he.'

'Is that legal?' Theo queried.

'In Ghana here we do what we want.'

Weaving through the arteries of the delta, they arrived at a sandy, brown bank. Winston reached out his hand, warning Theo about the alligators, and the philosopher stepped onto land. Johnson followed him and Winston into the bush. Winston began making hissing noises and clicking his fingers and the foliage thinned into desert. Three hours passed with no luck and Theo became dehydrated. Johnson muttered to himself and picked up sticks and waved them around while Winston continued, hissed and watched the sand. Occasionally, they would come across snake tracks – unconnected indentations where the snake hops across – but these faded with the blowing sand. Evening approached and Theo asked Johnson if Jah would provide any water. Johnson laughed and kicked stones or else made a peculiar observation. There were occasional false alarms when Winston would jolt still but when he moved the shrub aside he would see a rat or grass snake. Although Theo had struggled so hard to commence the gathering process, his dizzy exhaustion and the presence of darkness cast an ominous shadow on their business. The emergence of scorpions and creatures of the night coupled with no liquid supplies put Theo into a mild panic.

'Chaleh? You look not irie,' said Johnson.

'Yes, I'm feeling a bit dishevelled. I am pretty dehydrated. We need water and, well, we've been walking for hours. Do you think we are going to find the blasted thing?' Johnson nodded and asked Winston in Twi if they were close and Winston sucked his teeth and spoke for a minute. Johnson nodded again and turned to Theo.

'He tink dere are cobra but is hard to find. Dere is no way of knowing exactly where. Dis is da problem here.'

'Perhaps we should come back another time,' sighed Theo. 'It's not worth killing ourselves over. I really can't hike on much longer.'

'You want to return home?' Johnson questioned.

'Yes. Yes I do.' said Theo glumly.

'We come all dis way?'

'It's dangerous. We have no water and are in the middle of the jungle.'

'Dis like da pumpkin!' Johnson exclaimed. 'Click. Such is white man's patience.' Winston inquired what was being said and Johnson told him. He also sighed at Theo's feeble stamina but despite the philosopher's reluctance to give up, a pounding headache and eccentric heartbeat rendered further questing impossible.

'Let us turn back. I think I'm going to die,' he announced five minutes later. Annoyed and disappointed, Winston and Johnson turned around and headed back to the canoe. The fact that they were heading towards water and away from scorpions was a source of relief for Theo but his waving of the white flag confirmed what he had feared all along; that he was not cut out for this mission. He had fumbled at the first hurdle and wondered how in God's name he was going to pull this off. Winston rowed them over the lake and Johnson thanked him for his effort, slipping him some cash. Johnson and Theo hiked round the Kakum and bought two plastic bags of water from a stall. Theo gulped it down like a fish and Johnson sipped his.

'I'm very sorry,' said Theo. 'I feel terrible.'

'No problem,' said Johnson. 'I just thought you needed to gather.'

'I do. I have to find some other way of getting hold of it. Perhaps we can look at the market or I could get one on ebay.' Johnson recommended they head to the tro-tro and try to get back to Mamprobi that night. Hydrated and relaxed, Theo agreed. Two hours later they arrived at the stop and sat on the sand until the Accra tro-tro arrived with no seats and one square wheel.

'Chaleh... we back,' whispered Johnson some hours later. Theo shook his head awake and they walked grimily through the midnight streets of the capital. Johnson headed for his mother's house where Theo could find the food, water and floorboard lacking from the Jerusalem classroom. Johnson made him a bed on her comfortable sofa and brought him another pint of water.

III

The sound of dishes clinking and soup bubbling awoke Theo the next morning. For a few moments he wondered why he was not in his bed in Cambridge, but he soon remembered. Johnson's mother, an elderly gaunt woman with few teeth, sang gospel songs to herself while preparing lunch. Through the thin curtain Theo squinted to see Johnson practising his kicks while deep voices sounded from nearby. Theo stretched his arms and sat up on the sofa. Johnson's mother called out and Johnson stepped through the curtains and grinned at Theo.

'How?'

'Not bad,' said Theo, shielding his eyes from the rays of early sun. 'Better in fact.'

'My mother make us good breakfast. For me and you, and also my uncle and friends. Come to meet dem outside if you want, when you ready.'

'Is there a shower around?' asked Theo, who had not cleaned himself with moving water since his arrival.

'No shower. Some bucket if you want.'

'Never mind.'

'So come to meet uncle.'

'I'm not feeling too sociable right now.'

'I think if you are interested to see something den you should come to meet uncle and his friends becar dey are something important, especially Joe.'

'Okay,' sighed Theo. Johnson led him through the open doorway where a long bench was nailed to the side of the house and eight podgy middle-aged men sat in the sweet shade playing a board game whilst having earnest conversations. The game was *adubi* which was a cross between snatch, chess and draughts. At first they would zoom their pieces around the board so fast it was impossible to tell whose go was when. It then slowed and towards the end could take an hour to make a move. Johnson introduced Theo to everyone and they raised their hands and tapped the bench with their knuckles; a faded, hard bench worn under the weight of chubby bottoms over a million space hours. Johnson returned to help his mother and Theo sat back and waited for breakfast. There were long stretches of silence, a chat flared into a debate, arms flailed and the volume leapt up to laughter followed by the waving of hands, the slap of a thigh and the original quiet. They were in the middle of an argument as Theo sat down, in fact.

'It is da logic!' marvelled Charles. 'If I say mah mother works for KLM airlines and you come to house and see no uniform or clue you see I lying.'

'How can you believe from preaching? Where is proof?' asked Affo.

'What is the debate over?' asked Theo.

'Teachin' versus Preachin',' said the skinny, hard Kobi.

'I sleep – God – and I wake – God. Who else?'

'But I listen to teacher but faith no question – fact. Preacher no fact no question.'

'Excuse me one minute,' interrupted Kobi. 'You are not understanding one thing. It is not everybody who can inquire into knowledge, are you getting me? To impart is something.'

'Who cannot impart is lazy!' shouted Johnson from inside the house.

'Preaching is hope, teaching mud,' announced Charles.

'My noble friends of Christian faith,' sighed Affo. 'Christ was both preacher and teacher.'

'Personally I see distinction,' mused Albert. 'In teaching the student is given the chance to question but in preaching no.' Seeing Theo's bemusement, the fattest of the men shuffled over, patted him on the shoulder and said 'Wah!' which sounded like 'war' but was actually just a sonic exclamation mark, or verbal affirmation that the universe is indeed here. Joe wore a large fluffy beanie hat and had slightly pointy eyes. He was the local healer, collecting tree bark from nearby wooded areas for a malarial cure which he and Kobi brewed in a black cauldron. It is difficult to say what Joe and his friends were. They were not lazy bums. They were basically waiting in space. On the worn bench they observed nature. Their philosophy was a little vague, floaty and lacking in analytic rigour and there did not seem to be any sharp grid of scientific reason drawn up around nature. It breathed and tap-danced, mists clinging to trees and stars shimmering over still waters.

'You want to find out what in your soul?' asked Joe while the argument bounced behind him.

'Erm, well I suppose.' Theo replied. 'Do you know about those sorts of things?'

'Wah!'

'What?'

'Nature is so wonderful, I lie?'

'Yes, it's lovely.'

'I know what is on the stars, the planets.'

'No you don't,' said Theo firmly.

'Tree bode well for us. Ah feel it.'

'That isn't the same as seeing.'

'Wah!' A small boy ran out and spoke in Twi, and the chaps clapped their hands and walked to the other side of the house where a large table lay prepared beneath a tall nut tree and Johnson assisted his mother in laying out the food.

'What's for breakfast, Johnson?' asked the famished Englishman as everyone assembled around the table.

'You like the cat?' asked Johnson.

'Yes. My family have two.'

'Two make big stew!'
'I'm sorry?'
'Come eat cat.'

'Oh dear,' sighed Theo, 'I misunderstood.' A tray of bowls was brought to the table and the boys sat down eagerly. Theo stared at the contents, the innards of cat soaked in yellow soup and chunks of yam soaking up the feline stew. He kept nibbling his corn sticks to stave off the inevitable but everyone stared at him. Bravely he reached his fingers in and lifted a congealed lump towards his mouth. It was raw and bloody, the smell of deceased cat mingling with the heat, sewage and constant odour of boiling milk. As he chewed the fat and the men watched him expectantly he went through his six times table like a mantra. His throat occasionally went into spasms of aversion as if to say 'No'. After three more mouthfuls he sat back and said, 'Boy, am I stuffed!' The woman pleaded for Theo to eat more since she was concerned about his low body weight but Theo maintained that he was done and that it was precisely his low body weight that allowed him to get to Africa via the fifth dimension in the first place.

'So Teo and myself must return to beach,' said Johnson, sensing that Theo was feeling queasy and needing to lie down.

'Come and go,' pleaded Joe. 'Return soon and we find out ya soul!'

'Certainly,' agreed Theo. The men clapped and wished Theo well as he and Johnson hit the road and headed back to the Jerusalem classroom.

'Ah, you think well of Joe?' asked Johnson.

'A good chap yes. I'd like to go back and see what he's got to say about my soul because to be honest I don't know much about it myself. I'm feeling ill, but when I'm better I'd like to go back to find out about my soul. Because I am not sure about it.'

'What do you mean?'

'Well, I sometimes feel a curious movement, a nod towards a hidden depth. I'd like to give it more attention.'

'Take reefer,' said Johnson handing Theo a small bag of gem, 'I go for training.' Johnson had concluded that Theo could conquer many lands but taekwondo would not be one. Theo thanked him both for the reefer and for letting him off more pumpkin kicking.

'Johnson, I'm sorry again. Are you still – I mean, there are other things I need to gather. I suppose you probably don't want to help now.'

'I help. I said I help you so I help you. But I tink you must go away and tink about bravery becar otherwise you always back out. I will help you but you must go and become stronger in will and den come back to me, okay?'

'Okay. One more thing. Are there any internet cafés around?'

'Yes. In Osu where we walk through before tro-tro. Remember?'

'Vaguely,' said Theo. 'Thanks Johnson. For everything.'

'No problem.'

The Englishman followed the long road back to Chaplain via Osu and, finding the small internet café, logged on to his account and was glad to see an email from Spinny. He and Calvin were laying low in Mexico and seemed in good spirits. Theo wrote that the project was running smoothly and the apparent meanness of the universe had lifted leaving pure synchronicity. A complete fib – Theo had so far gathered diddly-squat and that wasn't going to change any time soon. That being said, he was making small spiritual developments of his own which would only increase his chances of progress and, contented with that thought, he paid the man and kicked sand along the beach until hearing Chaplain's guitar and Garvey singing impromptu lyrics that went;

> No woman
> Be a trader
> Sellin'
> Better dan a boat
> A goat
> No no woman no cry
> Yeah
> Oh I if a pocket
> Better dan a moat
> Oh Lord I remember toward da woman
> Oh cry better lordy
> She was better dan a moat

Theo extracted a splinter of wood from the table and placed it in his satchel. The snowball had started. Next time he saw Johnson he would explain the project and be ready to fight for it with courage, to blitz through the country braving rain or shine. Jung claimed the magnet of the soul attracts circumstances of the same frequency. If Theo's soul was trembling, how could he expect to seize bold treasures? Over the last few months Theo had caught fractured glimpses of that beacon – the soul that is – but its colour was still monochromed by his over-reliance on conscious, clean thought. Perhaps Joe could blow away the veil and introduce Theo to the rainbow of now and connect him internally. While waiting for Joe to get things ready he could also work through the Taoist manual. When he returned to the Jerusalem classroom and went to collect it from *The Beagle*, the pod was nowhere to be seen. Someone had moved it from the storage place, and Theo ran to Chaplain in a panic.

'Chaplain! Where is my pod?'

'Oh, Teo how? I thought you leave. Tafari ask if he can take it and I say yes.'

'You what?' exclaimed Theo.

'You disappear after tune and I tink you had gone. So Tafari ask if he can take it and I see no problem.'

'Christ, you have to get it back. Where does Tafari live?'

'Just dere,' said Chaplain gesturing to a nearby hut were Tafari was sitting in *The Beagle* rocking it from side to side in an attempt to make it lift off. Theo ran over and banged on the canopy and Tafari opened it.

'Get out,' demanded Theo.

'Aw, I want to keep it,' said Tafari.

'Well you can't. That is my ticket home.' Tafari stepped out of *The Beagle* reluctantly and Theo wheeled it back to his room and said, 'Please don't do that again.'

'So this tune,' Chaplain went on, 'Our tune together, recall?'

'Yes,' sighed Theo with a thumping heart.

'Laurie thinks we can make it. Laurie is Garvey brother.'

'I haven't got time,' said Theo, who had resolved to keep focused on the project and not be sidetracked into whirlpools such as the recording that Chaplain was suggesting.

'But Teo – only small effort and tink – you liked the tune. Garvey him say could sell like fire!'

'It is a good tune,' admitted Theo.

'So why no?' Theo wanted to say that he must work on the project, but feared another outburst of shouting. Perhaps it wouldn't be so bad to get a few rehearsals together, and if they could shift some copies it would bring the vicars into some cash which they certainly deserved.

'Okay,' said Theo. 'In spare moments I am willing to help. Is there somewhere to record?'

'Me brudder have studio,' said Garvey.

'Really?'

'Yes.'

'So shall we contact him?

'Yah.'

'How much will it cost? And don't say Jah will provide, because that guy is all mouth and no trousers.'

'Depend on time, but also need to find engineer,' Garvey said professionally.

'Why an engineer?' queried Theo.

'Make sound irie. Udderwise no irie.'

'Who is the engineer?'

'Also brudder. Laurie.'

'So when should we start?'

'Let me go see Laurie but I think Saturday, say, four in da sun?'

'Yes. Four o clock.'

'Chaplain?' asked Theo.

'Irie.'

'So four o'clock on Saturday afternoon?' Garvey smiled.

'Laurie good and make sound right,' said Chaplain.

'Yes, so we'll meet on Saturday at four.' Theo knew this arrangement would be chaos, but wanted to offer them something for putting him up, feeding him. He spent the night trying to cultivate bravery in various ways, mostly by visualizing himself in some act of astonishing courage and nodding at it, and by the time he fell asleep he had genuinely increased his mettle. He headed to Johnson's place the next morning to see if they could make it down to Kumasi for the weed, but the wily headcase was nowhere to be seen.

'Ah!' popped Joe. 'You return. Good. I have prepared.'

'Is Johnson here?'

'No. Johnson training on beach.'

'Oh right.'

'You want to know soul?'

'Erm, well I really need to speak to him. It's urgent.'

'But in meanwhile?'

'Okay, yes,' agreed Theo. Joe's face was wide and excited. 'While I wait I guess. How do we do it?'

'Come. Ba,' and Joe stood up, slipped his sandals on and led Theo around the back of the house towards a slab of concrete surrounded by four brick walls where Kobi was stirring some buckets of water. Joe told Theo to take his clothes off.

'Off?'

'Yes. Off.'

'Is there somewhere to change?'

'Here. Change here.'

'Er, can you turn around or something?'

'Teo, take off da clothes and stand inside walls,' Joe laughed. Reluctant, Theo removed everything except his underpants and walked onto the slab and took off his underpants and threw them over.

'Good. Kobi bring buckets of water. You pour over you and scrub skin wit' gristly sponge here, all skin – pour over head as well. Finished give small whistle and Kobi bring another. You do twelve bucket and den we find out about ya soul.' Theo stood naked in the heat and Kobi brought the first bucket. The water was light green with dusts and leaf-clippings floating and twigs at the bottom. He poured it over his head and down his body and then washed with the sandpaper sponge. After the dregs were finished he whistled and Kobi brought him the second bucket. The liquid dried quickly and left him feeling fresh-minty. At the bottom of the last bucket he noticed a twig and his soul quivered. The testicle breathing had reconnected Theo to his subconscious and he sensed it was a bancha twig. The ablution had cleared the way for bio-cosmic intuition, which is an awfully handy paranormal phenomena to have on your side in these sorts of missions.

'Wait,' said Kobi, walking towards Joe. Theo shook his hair dry and stood cool in the heat with the bancha twig in his fist. Kobi waved for Theo to enter a side room adjoined to the house. He put on the cotton trousers Kobi had left for him and followed Joe along the corridor. Joe's sandals shuffled along the stone floor as he passed a low-roofed doorway and entered a sparse room with a square window where a fat woman dressed in white lay on a mattress wriggling around with her eyes half-closed. She was mumbling and making strings of words, discordant melodies and bird noises. Joe pointed to a small chair and Theo sat down. After half an hour of sitting in silence Theo got peeved. It was nearly five o'clock and he was still none the wiser as to the nature of his soul and Johnson may have been back soon to get him to Kumasi.

'So are we going to do this stuff or what?' he asked. Joe nodded and spoke to the woman in Twi. She fixed her eyes on Theo and began writhing on the bed, kicking the wall and working herself into a trance. Joe questioned her and she spoke in broken sentences which Joe translated.

Apparently, Theo's former soul was that of a freedom fighter renowned for his bravery who was ambushed and killed by his own men. Since his murder had been one of betrayal, his soul was still in unresolved exile at the place of his death; a dark secluded cave in the mountains of Spain where three olive trees entwined. Theo had to eliminate the residue of wickedness that had clung to his soul through its later incarnations by performing an act of love and bravery in the same cave. She went on to recall accurate information about the six moles on Theo's bottom which were dotted in the shape of the Andromeda formation, and finally she conked out and began snoring.

'So Teo, you must bring soul forward. Dis is da power dat pushes birds over de oceans.'

'Does it?'

'White man concerned with clear thinking. In Ghana here we tink muddled becar da soul is muddled. The muddled soul is da power dat pushes birds across de ocean.' The room was hot. 'See how da nature manifest in de inner process. Do not think too much of books or other people thought. You well schooled in udder people's thought but not yar own. True thought bubble up from inside with da same power dat pushes birds across ocean.'

'But when I try to introspect, I see nothing.'

'Eh, you can't see anything just like man who comes into black cave is blind – he can't see anything but den eyes quiet and he can see more and more and when he come outside again the tiniest light so bright.'

'Mmm, that is interesting. Really interesting stuff.'

'Do not make it something to include in ya reservoir of knowledge. Make it base of thought.'

'Thanks, Joe.'

'No problem. Wah!' Theo stood up and thanked the woman and as he returned to the bench to say goodbye to the waiters he saw Johnson cooling off and dabbing his torso with a towel.

'Hi Johnson,' said Theo, his voice suddenly sounding a little deeper as is the case when the soul becomes active.

'Teo, I can see some new enthusiasm. You speak with Joe?'

'Yes.'

'Good,' said Johnson, who clipped Theo on the ear.

'Say Johnson, is this a bancha twig?' he asked showing Johnson the twig he had pulled out of the bucket.

'Yes. It is.'

'Okay,' said Theo smugly. 'So all I need now is the jimson weed and—'

'Eh Teo, can we speak another time about it?' tutted Johnson. 'I want to ask you for some favour now. Mutual benefit!'

'Sure. What's wrong?'

'I was tinking about tings becar you are on dis project but we are still here. So I had an idea. I was tinking I could start bicycle taxi service. I will get bicycle and attach new seat and take people – cheaper dan taxi. Den I will be strong for taekwondo and make money.'

'Sounds like a nice idea. They do that in India I think. There was a program about it on Discovery.'

'But you see, I have so small money and I working occasionally.'

'But you studied. I mean, you have a degree. Can't you find

better work?'

'I not finished degree. I leave some way through, multiple reasons. Bicycle is best, but dere is problem.'

'What is it?'

'Da bicycle I looking at cost 30,000 cedis – about thirty of ya pounds.'

'I can probably help you out with that,' said Theo, since Calvin had contributed several hundred dollars to the trip, yet with the generosity Theo was receiving he might not require such funds.

'Really?'

'Sure. It's the least I can do after last week.'

'Oh very kind. Maybe I come in morning to fetch it? I want to reserve bicycle,' said Johnson, his eyes lighting up.

'Sure,' said Theo. 'Now can we speak about this project?'

'Of course! Next week we finish. Do not worry. I make inquiry. You will be finished here next week I am sure. I will now dedicate myself to you.' Johnson ran towards Accra and Theo walked as if in a trance through the melting streets which exhaled as the night came in. The sun hung red and waxy, shimmering over the roof of smoggy Accra and Theo watched the ball of peace turn as he walked to the Jerusalem classroom full of the power that pushes the birds across the oceans.

IV

In the two days that followed he worked through some more of his sexual techniques, checked emails and rehearsed with Chaplain. Theo had faith that Johnson would bring his work here to closure so long as he remained brave. There were frequent soul stirrings, and as for the tune it was touching upon greatness. When Saturday arrived Theo, Tataguan and Chaplain set off after a *kenke* lunch with the guitar and scoresheet to Laurie's place, one of eight shanty houses leaning against each other in a circle around a sandy square yard. They arrived a few minutes before four and nobody was home. Theo immediately became peeved.

'Oh,' said Chaplain, sitting by the step and fiddling with his dreadlocks while women swept their porches and infants threw small things against walls.

'Where are they?' asked Theo, looking through the windows and knocking on all the doors.

'Relax chaleh. Be here soon.'

'I knew this would happen,' he sighed, pacing around. Chaplain began dozing and Theo kicked dust agitatedly.

'You know this would never happen in Switzerland,' moaned the philosopher.

'Dere are udder tings dat also not happen in Switzerland,' said Chaplain.

'Yes, I suppose that is true.'

'Why don't you grow da dreadlocks?' asked Tataguan, resting back on the clay bricks of the neighbours' front wall.

'Dreadlocks? No I couldn't possibly.'

'I tink would look good on you Teo. Give you some lion,' Tataguan urged, to Chaplain's amusement.

'I think, well, I think I would look a bit silly, you know, returning to Cambridge with dreadlocks.'

'Me apologies,' came a voice as a carbon copy of Garvey emerged from over the road with Garvey next to him. 'Pleased to meet you. I am Laurie.'

'Hi. I'm Theo.'

'Chaplain, how?'

'Irie.'

'Tataguan?'

'Aish.'

'Come.' The five of them entered the locked studio. Three mikes stood on solid stands, two without pop shields, and an eight-track mixing desk was perched on a table covered in crumbs. A forlorn drum kit sat in the corner and there were two large amps, one with a hole in it and the wires poking out.

'Right,' said Laurie swiping the crumbs from the mixing desk. 'What instruments are we thinking about?'

'Guitar, mandolin, *djembe*,' said Theo.

'And tin whistle!' piped Garvey. Theo looked taken aback.

'We are not having a tin whistle on the track,' he said firmly.

'How no tin whistle? We have to have!' exclaimed Garvey.

'I'm sorry we cannot put a tin whistle on this song. It will be melancholy and emotive. I can't see what a tin whistle could possibly contribute.'

'But we have one, so why not use it?'

'You don't put an instrument on a tune just because you've got it.'

'Some conflict here,' observed Laurie.

'I know someone with bass drum,' said Tataguan.

'We need two toms,' added Chaplain.

'Nat fair! I do not understand why only my instrument cannot be on track!'

'Does seem unfair, Teo,' agreed Laurie.

'But I want to pitch the warm vocal against a grainy rhythm section. I can't see where the tin whistle will fit into that vision.'

'Why your vision?' asked Garvey.

'Heck okay, why not get some cow-bells and tambourines in there as well?' Theo asked.

'I 'ave friend serious on tambourine,' said Tataguan.

'You know Teo, I tink tin whistle might fill out sound,' Chaplain mused.

'Fill out the sound? Whoever heard of putting a tin whistle on an arrangement to fill out the sound?'

'But it could give air of original to separate us from da Marley,' Chaplain went on. 'We need to find our own place in da hall of greats.'

'Let's take it one step at a time, shall we?'

'Vote seems to be against you, white man,' said Laurie, and Theo realized nobody had come in on his side. Fearing that he might create tension in the atmosphere, he surrendered. Laurie said he would set up the studio to start recording on Monday. Before then two of them would have to go into Accra market to buy a new deer skin for the *djembe*. As the only one with money, Theo agreed to go with Tataguan on Sunday morning. The band dispersed and Theo returned with the vicars in a slightly jaunty mood, still not sure about this idea but confident in Johnson's assurance that it would all be wrapped up in a week. After a bean and yam dinner Theo sat by as the vicars prayed and looked at the cuts of white on the distant waves.

He and Tataguan took a taxi into Accra the next morning.

By eleven the sun was strong and Tataguan led them around in circles looking for the deer skin stall. Tataguan and Theo got a bit miffed with each other because Tataguan kept buying yams or talking to beautiful girls and calling them 'Empress'. Theo demanded they just find the stall and buy the deer skin before things became uncomfortably hot. They reached an animal hide stall at midday where one of Tataguan's friends worked. They explained their requirement and he nodded and walked off. An hour later he returned and smiled at them and sat back down. When Theo queried where the skin was he said 'Oh! I forget. I go and come.'

'Forget it,' said Theo, and he marched out. This tardiness was still infuriating. Back in his days writing computer manuals, Theo had become used to bending life to his whim at speed. With axioms and logic the disparate fragments of the world could be compressed into lightning, yet this clumsy world of the macro was sticky and congested. It was not smart/digital nor clean/quantum.

Tataguan brought them to a larger animal hide store where an old man stood up, leaning forward and occasionally tiptoeing with his small belly poking out under his eighties Manchester United T-shirt. Tataguan spoke and the man walked them to a line of silvery grey skins. Tataguan ran his fingers down them, smelt and prodded them. He nodded at each one and finally came back to the second skin.

'Teo, dis one is best. Tight. Need be tight so 'pop', but also not too dry so you get warm sound udderwise too dusty.'

'If too old sound flat but if too new soft,' added the old man, smiling a no-teeth smile at Theo.

'How much?' asked Theo, cutting to the chase. The old man said 40,000 cedis, roughly forty pounds. It seemed out of proportion. Theo told Tataguan they were being fleeced. Tataguan told the old man who grumbled. Theo apologized, haggled and bartered and finally settled for 35,000 and the man unhooked the deer skin and Tataguan threw it over his shoulder. The two of them worked their way out of the chaos and followed the beach road to Mamprobi.

Chaplain took the skin from them and examined it, laying a bag of condiments on the table. First he set fire to the hairs and smothered it out once the patch was bald. To eliminate stubble he covered the skin in shaving foam and took his razor to it and then dropped small blobs of gin from a green bottle which evaporated, imbuing the skin with vibes. It lay in the afternoon sun for two hours while Chaplain and Tataguan lead some chants to vibrate the skin up to Rastafarian frequencies. Ready and poised, Chaplain cut the shape and spread it over the *djembe*.

Theo headed to Johnson's place to see if he had a game-plan for the remaining elements but the old boys had not seen him that day. Joe asked how his soul was feeling and Theo said when he left the medium it had come into view but he had become disgruntled and irritable again. Joe said to keep watching. Theo agreed and said he would keep Joe informed and requested he tell Johnson to swing by the Jerusalem classroom.

The band headed to the studio after lunch on Monday. Theo had prepared himself for technical disasters and hours of waiting but when they arrived Laurie had set everything ready. Peter Tosh posters were nailed to the walls and a sack of weed lay open. Garvey had brought his tin whistle. Chaplain seated himself comfortably by the mike and the others took their positions, ran some scales and practised the tune. Laurie took rough recordings to get the sound levels and textures integrated and there was much tweaking, moving of mikes here, raising them there, muffling of amps and facing of drums against the wall to attain sonic socialism. Some small structural changes were also made to the tune after Chaplain accidentally played a dominant 5th and made the bridge more optimistic, and a new half-verse was sandwiched between the solo and the chorus. Despite disagreements and uncertainties, progress was forwardy and after supper they decided to get a good night of sleep before the final take.

The vicars and Theo strolled back to the studio the following afternoon on a cloud of complacency, picking up their instruments and starting to play with bifters dangling from their lips. To their surprise and woe, they sounded pants. Thin, grainy and clumsily played, the tune had lost its warm sexy grace.

'Gosh,' sighed the philosopher. 'Yesterday it was sounding so good. What is wrong with us?'

'Too arrogant,' admitted Chaplain. 'We need to be honest again – honest and play together.' Laurie recommended they break or return the next day but Theo was reluctant to quit. He feared a gloom would hang over the tune. Chaplain agreed and they pressed on but only became more scattered. Tataguan kept singing the wrong part or the right part in the wrong place. He often came in with the backing mirror vocal to 'how long' when Chaplain sang 'strange'. It was supposed to go:

| (how long) | (straiange) |
| 'how long | You gonna live in a strange land |

NOT

| | (how long) |
| 'how long | You gonna live in a strange land |

Tafari meanwhile, who was not even supposed to be on the tune, kept doing his stupid 'krang krang' noise, convinced that it was indistinguishable from wah-wah guitars, while Garvey released piercingly discordant tin whistle toots at any instant that he pleased and halfway through a decent take he suddenly shouted, 'Da white man's time is over!' which did not go down too well since Theo was paying for the session.

'No Garvey!' admonished Chaplain. 'No politics. We make toon. Quiet da racism.'

'And the tin whistle,' mumbled Theo. His D string then fell a semitone out while Tataguan went into Dionysian euphoria, thrashing the drumsticks around in a closed-eye mania and snapping the drumstick. Laurie sank his head onto the mixing desk. Laurie's wife arrived with a tray of food and everyone lay down their instruments and gathered round.

'Ah,' sighed Theo, when handed his bowl of gruel, 'more *fufu*.' The musicians ate and chatted. They spoke of women, lofty plans and God. Fingers were soaked in soup-stodge, banana skins balanced on symbols and more crumbs of corn wedged into the grooves of the mixing desk. After their bellies were filled Chaplain put his bowl aside and began noodling on the guitar, Tafari quietly humming and Tataguan sitting up on his stool and tocking. Theo took up his mandolin and winked at Laurie, who blew the crumbs away and pushed the microphones up to begin recording.

Theo gave a count and they whacked out 'Thousands of Letters' with considerable verve. In fact the performance was so vervy that Tataguan, lost in the swirl of music, brought down his other unbroken drumstick with an over-zealous thwack and pierced the deer skin. 'Oh no!' gasped Tafari, making his lips into an 'O' shape. Everyone stopped playing but with the reels still turning Theo invented an impromptu solo while the boys stretched the skin out and wound it around the *djembe*. Hushed voices and vigorous pointing followed but as Theo brought back the motif the band took up their instruments and headed unified into the final chorus.

'That is a ruddy hit!' exclaimed Theo, and no one disagreed. Laurie shook his head in reverence for the recording with its analogue authenticity and vintage crackliness. They blazed the rest of the weed and slept on the floor, awakening early the next morning to begin mastering and mixing. There was still some disagreement over the tin whistle but apart from the most agonizing parts, Theo conceded and left it in. This was despite several attempts to accidentally delete Garvey's part by performing very elaborate sequences of movements meant to constitute the act of falling over next to the mixing desk and dragging the volume of the tin whistle track down with him. A few things flew around the studio but a resolution was made. Chaplain and Tataguan took the burn into Accra with yet more of Theo's diminishing funds and pressed it onto vinyl, while the philosopher, dimly reminded of his responsibilities, returned to the Jerusalem classroom to sleep and track down Johnson the following day.

V

As he set off the next morning with a splitting headache to Johnson's mother, Tataguan jumped on his back. He and Chaplain delivered the tune to a radio station in Accra who told them about a reggae festival in Kumasi that afternoon. 'Thousands of Letters' had already received considerable airplay the previous night and they were advised to get on the circuit and throw their work to the people. Theo refused. He had to maintain autonomy instead of being continually swept up in activities that served to distract him from his work, yet Tataguan pleaded with him to come and play since the band were nothing without their lead mandolinist, at which point Theo suddenly recalled that Kumasi was the home of jimson weed. He changed tack sharp, agreed and they caught a taxi, swinging by Laurie's place to pick up the instruments and the band and bolting to Kumasi, a two-hour drive. As they arrived at the fishing town they saw a cloud of smoke and a thousand dreadlocked heads. The band, who Chaplain had now christened 'The Jerusalem Vicars and the Atheist', settled at the periphery while Tafari pushed his way to the main stage and put their names down to perform. After several hours of chaotic organization, the festival began as a tall Rastafarian approached the mike.

'Ladies and Guys, Rastafari!' There was mass cheering and clapping. Foot-long spliffs poked triumphantly into the air. 'Welcome to festival. Come sign up at the front and winner of festival be getting much weed. First up, Rasta Pasta!' Rasta Pasta took the stage and dropped in with dub delays. Tafari listened closely to the sound of wah-wah guitars to improve his technique while the others prepared themselves for the performance. Theo ran through his scales, ready to play his guts out for the prize and bring himself to within one element of completion. After five mediocre reggae performances The Jerusalem Vicars and the Atheist were called up. At first there was animosity at the sight of Theo's pale face. Some people shouted, 'Go home whitie!' and others threw tomatoes at him, yet when he rocked in with that killer riff and Chaplain leaned up close to the mike, ears cocked towards them. It took only half a verse before silence fell upon the audience and a thousand faces gazed at Chaplain as he sang 'Is it better to believe or to learn to know?' Sexy muffin sellers swooned at him, and when Theo stepped up for his solo jaws dropped. As the final E sharp resolved, the audience mauled in pulsations of religious ecstasy and reached their hands to touch the band as they stepped off the stage, Garvey even stopping to sign autographs. The festival organizers handed them the satchel of jimson weed and they pushed through the crowds to smoke it. People took it in turns to congratulate them and ask when the EP was out. Chaplain became the spokesperson and compiled a fan mailing list. The chap at the Accra radio station told them he was heading back to the studio and they should listen in for their review.

    They immediately shot up, headed for the road and hailed for a cab – the only way they could catch the review out there. They told him to circle round until the review, and Theo would pay for the trip. Half an hour later and with a few thousand cedis notched on the metre, they started the review.

    'So now we move to our music wit Clement... Clement?' There was silence and shuffling and the hushed whispering of 'Clement! Get over here!'

    'Yeah, hi cats, well I just rolled in from Reggae Festival Kumasi and wanted to tell you bout new band who will be receiving much attention. Dey drop a tune off here only yesterday, and we already see greatness. Dey are called 'Da Yerusalem Vicars and Da Atheist' and they just won the Kumasi Festival wit deir debut single 'Thousands of Letters.' Now dere are few noteworthy things of this tune. Firstly da mandolin solo – almost sounds accidental, as though it wasn't supposed to be dere. Dis is a special, awkward effect dat is very hard to master. I myself have tried it on guitar to no avail. Very proficient all tha same, even if it is played by a funkless whitie. Da vocal and harmony deep and harmonious, very irie, and de front man has considerable appeal for da lady! I myself have been trying to achieve this for some years but to no avail. HOWEVER da most outstanding element of da tune, what really was beauty and stamp it as original is da genius whistle! Oh! So windy sound, so pure and unexpected, coming in at strange and carefully considered moments. Dis shows deir willingness to move away from classic interpretation and reinvent reggae.' Eveyone laughed, Garvey stared out of the window with that quiet nobility of the stoic which implies 'first they laugh at you, then they ignore you, then they fight you then you win'. 'So congratulations guys, and I am sending tune to some friends around the world to put Ghana here on da map!'

VI

When Theo awoke his head felt as though it was being crushed in a vice and his inner climate was arctic and equatorial. The band was nowhere to be seen. Chaplain and Tataguan were pressing up more records in Accra and Garvey was walking the streets to see if anyone recognised him. A swim in the sea changed nothing and Theo's temples soon pulsed in a fever so hot he pressed his head against an adobe wall for the coolness. By midday his condition worsened and he stumbled to the main road, hailed a cab and directed it to Johnson's mother's place in order to find out where the best hospital was. He fell out of the cab in delirium and Joe leapt up, picked him from the pavement and lay him down on a white bed. Chaotic thoughts ran wild in Theo's mind and the sheet was soon drenched in sweat. Suffering aches and nausea, he would have done anything to lie in light, to recline in the balance of sunshine, yet his fever and squashed head worsened.

Joe returned some moments later and soaked Theo's sizzling forehead with a piece of cloth soaked in aloe, handing Theo a glass of black juice which the philosopher drank in one gulp. His temperature falling, he was soon enveloped in sleep for two days. Lions, breasts and bloody skies filled his dreams, the epic inscape peopled with omen-heavy words from invisible corners. A sense of doom pressed in as though the creatures of the bush cast warnings yet nodded towards the weight of darkness. Theo, dimly aware of himself in the dreams, decided not to venture into that lair of humidity and danger and in the moments where he shuddered awake he readied himself to move on. The dreams weakened and his conscious mind regained the reigns, bringing him to awareness as he came through the worst of the malaria. He spent the afternoon stroking his chest hairs and picking bits of food that Joe had left for him by the bed. Although he had tried to save the corn sticks, he was soon down to the last one and as he contemplated the final bite, Johnson knocked.

'Come in,' said Theo and Johnson paced in.

'Some sickness? Whitey came thru.'

'Maybe not as weak as you thought, eh?' said Theo.

'I think you lucky for Joe. Him cure are never fallibled. Malaria normally very long, but you just big confused sleep den recovering. Joe very special.'

'Yes. Is he around?'

'He play *adubi*.'

'Oh.'

'Eh, you like da monkey tail, eh?' chuckled Johnson, nodding to the corn stick in Theo's hand.

'Monkey tail!' he shouted, spitting out a mouthful. 'I thought you said they were corn?'

'Oh yes. Corn. But we call them monkey tail, becar how dey look. Brown, straight den curl.'

'My oh my, so that's it then? I'm all done?'

'What?'

'I have only a monkey tail left, and here it is!' he squeaked.

'Good.'

'So listen Johnson,' Theo went on, feeling for the first time so far that this project might work. 'I am still a little unwell but as soon as I'm up and running I think I am going to skip out of here. My work is finished.'

'Ah yes. Not so wonderful any more?' he said sadly.

'Still wonderful, Johnson, but time is passing and I have much to get on with. Two more continents to cover.' Johnson made little attempt to hide his melancholy.

'Eh chaleh, I wonder on one last favour.'

'Sure.'

'I am thinking about my future and Ghana here hold nothing. I wonder if maybe I can make a go of de life in England. I visit Embassy and dey give me visa application. I have it here. And I fill out my part but need you as reference to say how I am and also dat you will be responsible for me in UK. I come here, though you sick, to ask you dis at some time before you leave.' Johnson's face was hopeful. It was a new plan and he approached it with a naïve belief, a constant mountain of renewable hope immune to the eroding winds and waves of reality – that great dream breaker.

'Right.'

'I have written me own letter telling why I am good citizen.'

'What is it you want to do in England?'

'I tink I can bring my martial art. We can set up dojo. Practise hall. You can do business and marketing, I do training. Me and you, Teo. How about it?'

'I don't know Johnson. I am happy to vouch for you but I can't guarantee you will make money in England and besides my future looks pretty uncertain too.'

'Let us just try, eh? Here are forms,' and he handed Theo the green and white papers. 'So maybe we can start on letter?' Theo lay back. He still felt dazed. The skinny warrior was itching to get on. 'Tell me what you think of this... Dear Sir, May da Lord God Bless You—'

'Eh, I'm not sure about that,' sighed Theo.

'What?'

'That isn't really how we start formal letters in England.'

'How do you start?'

'Normally like, 'Dear Sir, I am writing to request.' Johnson tutted.

'I tink it is not so friendly. Let us keep our one.'

'Okay. Go on.'

'I hope da life continue for you indefinitely.'

'Okay,' grinned Theo. 'Go on.'

'I am writing to request special favour in de name of Selassie I, Lion of Ethiopia, Jah! I have been bunning blaze...'

'Don't say you've been bunning blaze,' said Theo.

'Why not? We should start on note of truth.'

'Johnson, the British Embassy will not let you into England if you say you have been blazing illegal drugs.'

'Okay. I been praying – praying with noble TEO FINTWISTLE. I put in capitals. He is an irie ambassador for her majesty dem queenie republic in de highest. Anyhow, resources dem be in short supply becar Babylon on one side and bandits on other squash me into abject poverty. I be having serious dreams about future – chant down da wickedness like Joshua. I also want pod like da Fintwistle, and to meet Phil Collins. Anyway, I am waffling on. For these reasons I want to be granted citizenship in England. I sincerely ask you allow me and if possible me pals Chaplain and Tataguan – picture enclosed – to get three visas and come live with ya.' Mustering his strength, Theo signed on the dotted line. Johnson thanked him and promised to take Theo to dinner once he was better. He left and told Joe Theo was awake and recovering and Joe soon replenished his water. Theo thanked him for the care and the black liquid and Joe said 'Wah!'

One more night of decent and unperturbed sleep was enough to grind the malaria into dust, and Theo stood up and changed into some spare clothes. Joe and his buddies asked when he would come back to play *adubi*, and he said he had to move on. Disappointed, they patted his back and waved him off fondly as though he were another pin in the infinite sad sewing cushion of life. Joe advised him to keep an eye on his inner processes, and if he ever wanted to converse he should look at the planets swerving in rings and Joe would tune in. Johnson, dressed smart in a shirt and tie, met him by the beach that night and they headed off for dinner. Swatting mosquitoes along the way and relaxed in the warmth, little was said even after they arrived at the restaurant in Accra and took their places.

'Chaleh, I should thank you,' said Johnson breaking the curious but comfortable silence.

'Thank me? Crikey, I should thank you.'

'You make me happy here. Really come in and give me something, I cannot say what. Just some time we speak. In the tro-tro to Kakum I feeling close to you. I want to be real friends and it is hard to suppress feeling now that you have to go so soon.'

'I'd like to stay, Johnson, but I have to get off.'

'Of course. I know we can still be friends but I fear it will be disparate, eh?'

'I know what you mean.'

'I am stuck. I don't think da Embassy will like our letter.'

'I think you are probably right there. It's unlikely they will give you a visa, certainly not a permanent one. But it's worth a try.'

'It's hopeless for me.'

'Not at all. It's not so bad for you to stay here, is it?'

'All me plans get thwarted by Pope.'

'The Pope?'

'Dem Pope at Embassy.'

'They have nothing to do with the Pope, Johnson!' Theo laughed, but Johnson was not in the mood to be contradicted.

'Dey 'ave! Pope, Embassy worker, dey all part of same silent majority smashing me head into dust wit clipboards.'

'They are just doing their jobs.'

'Tss. All plans fail.'

'What happened with that bicycle thing?' Johnson sucked his teeth and looked down.

'Chaleh, I wanted to tell you ah,'

'What? What is it, chap, no need to look so glum.'

'Da money dat I ask for bicycle. Was not for bicycle.'

'Oh really?' asked Theo, a little put out but not surprised. The whole thing had seemed odd to him from the start.

'I in debts with some people and I have to pay dem off. I been borrowing for long time and finally I have to pay... de money of you I gave to him,' he finally blurted, hanging his head in shame.

'Oh dear.'

'I feel so low becar your money come to no good. No productive, just debt. Dead money.'

'Well it stopped you getting in trouble.'

'I lied to you and you gave me money for lie. DIS is unexcusable on my part.'

'Look, maybe you did lie but it's only money, Johnson, and I won't miss it. I'm disappointed for you. I want your ideas to take off. Don't worry about me, for God's sake.'

'I want to give you picture,' he went on, handing Theo a photo of Johnson in his full taekwondo outfit. 'I want you to remember Ghana here.'

'Yes.' They ate their lousy spaghetti in silence and, hands in pockets, returned to the Jerusalem classroom where Chaplain and Tataguan were arguing. Theo gathered his bits and prepared the pod, inserting the next batch of firefly fuel and putting in his earplugs.

'Well chaps, I'm off,' said Theo.

'Eh so! Be fuelled, Teo. You not go to America,' warned Chaplain with a stern wave of the finger.

'No,' said Theo. 'Viti Levu.'

'Where?'

'Somewhere in the Pacific I think.'

'Me second swimming pool!' joked Chaplain.

'Boi!' burst Tataguan. 'We keep you informed of musical developments. Da mandolin will be missed.'

'We'll sort something out.'

'Okay, Theo. Go and come.'

'Yes,' he said with a small lump forming in his throat, though not the kind he would look up in his 'Fatal Diseases' book. 'I'll go and come.' He took *The Beagle* from its hideout, told Tafari to get out and wheeled it down to the beach. With the canopy fastened and the lever pulled, he shot back into the fifth dimension

'So dat is how white man travel!' marvelled a fisherman, while Johnson waved Theo off sadly and Tataguan rolled up another disarmingly large bifter.

Raw Chi War

I

Theo bounced back into Being, and after dusting down his knobbly knees he surveyed the landscape. The sun beamed onto the sea and turned the somber navy ocean into a splashy lemon surface. Giant fronds drooped with blobs of rain amassing at the leaf tip while whizzy fluorescent geckos scampered up beefy twisted oak trunks. Humble olive trees grew from the black peaty soil and gazed up at the swooping condors gliding in the blue sky with smirks of arrogance and no immediate plans. Beneath these squeaks and shuffles lay a deep silence as old as Time itself.

As the first pangs of hunger growled, Theo began to wonder what he was going to have for dinner. The island seemed completely devoid of supermarkets, toilets and basic societal infrastructure. Theo spent several hours looking desperately for human life but was afraid to venture too far into the foliage in case a big grim ape bit him in the nads. He mostly just shouted 'Hello?' and ran back to the beach when he heard any rustling noises. Exhaustion finally got the better of him and after taking a shot glass of seawater he lay beneath a mustang tree, lulling himself to sleep by counting the horrific afflictions he might suffer in the night.

The mountainous front of the island stretched over Theo's awakening eyes the following morning: cracks and chasms scarred with sharp daggers and darts, acute spears and Chinese symbols jutting out into a dim bearded fog of cloud. He straightened the wheels of *The Beagle* and pulled the now forlorn pod up the hilly incline to gain a better view. Wine-stained clouds, meandering trees and the slalom dash of small birds made for pleasant viewing but not bread. His only option was to yell for help and so he released hefty war cries and, setting fire to some pages out of his academic notebook, created blocks of smoke at intervals, a trick he had learned watching a program about Native Indians on the Discovery channel. The smoke was his best chance of survival but as darkness fell the ghosts of carbon mingled with the blackness of night. As he let out one last roar he heard a voice telling him to shut up.

'Oh hello,' said Theo. 'Sorry for shouting.'

'No problem,' said the aboriginal man in the hazy light, his skin hardened and bronzed with matted hair hanging over tired but vital cheeks. 'What's the problem?'

'I'm in something of a pickle,' said Theo, relieved that the man spoke English. 'I arrived here yesterday to gather some materials from this Jurassic isle, but have not managed to find any settlements or people.'

'That's because there aren't any.'

'Right. Apart from you.'

'Yes.'

'Do you live here?'

'Yes.'

'Could you help me?'

'Certainly,' said the man after a moment of consideration. 'But tread gently, young man. You are walking upon a microbial turf of ancient lineage in a state of life-giving tremulation.'

'Okay,' said Theo, taking off his boots.

'And don't shout like that.'

'My apologies again,' said Theo, pulling *The Beagle* from behind the tree and wheeling it behind him with his other hand.

'What on earth is that?' asked the old man.

'Oh, it's just my quantum pod,' said Theo nonchalantly.

'Things have changed.'

Theo followed him into the tundra and inhaled deeply the vitality of mystery and weight. The wall of green vegetation eventually broke into a small clearing where a stony path had been laid around two huts of wild lupine, one of which housed a large terrapin. Simple utensils and plates of carved ebony were scattered around a bowl of murky water. Theo and the old man sat by a smouldering fire and the old man fed it kindling and heated some oil in one of the plates, occasionally staring at Theo.

'A little isolated here isn't it?' said the philosopher to break the silence.

'Exactly,' said the old man quietly, the oil beginning to pop and crackle.

'Are there any other people?'

'There is a small Buddhist temple on the other side.'

'So what do you do here?'

'Survive.'

'Have you lived here long?' The old man shrugged. 'You speak quite good English,' Theo went on. 'When I first saw you I assumed you were a savage or something.' The old man looked up and explained.

His name was Ashley Dashlazer, an ecological pragmatist dining with space on velvet beans, Indian snakeroot and toasted amaranth seeds. Dashlazer, of aristocratic background, was one of the earliest Westerners to discover kava kava[5], which he found on his travels to Fiji in 1923. He described it as a 'mind sweller packed to the brim with cool', and became the very first beatnik – quite ahead of his time. After several years of flying from Worcester to Fiji he disappeared shortly after the outbreak of World War II. Some people said he had committed suicide during a hallucination while others believed his plane ran aground but in fact he was here in Viti Levu. Despairing of war and industry he had retired into tropical solitude to see humanity for what it was; a spasm of loneliness avenging our amputation from the biosphere by striving for material glory at

---

[5] Kava kava – herb used among tribes to encourage communication in a relaxed, friendly way. Often administered when disagreements arise such as whether to hunt, fish or build spears. Other uses include: cementing friendship and lifting inhibition. It is a foul-smelling, astringent resin which is crushed and pulverized into a psychoactive beverage and drunk, instilling mellowness/easy talk. Kava kava is a cable car in which weary jungle dwellers ascend to the sublime spheres at the end of the week. Some go into epileptic trances, others report blinding visions. Some have terrible visions of demons and phantoms of the underworld but most sleep until Monday

the expense of the atmospheric roof, and as the pages of nature's library have been tossed into the bonfire of human vanity so too a thousand anti-oxidant stomach-calming aphrodisiac herbs have drifted like stardust down the fag-end of modernity. He was pronounced dead in 1945 at the then tender age of fifty.

'Fifty!' gasped Theo. 'That makes you over a hundred years old. How have you lived so long?'

'By not fussing,' he said, putting a few snails on the hot plate.

'I suppose it must be fairly healthy living somewhere natural like this,' observed Theo, having noticed the salutary effect the sweet oxygen was having on him. It was so nourishing that Theo had survived almost twenty-four hours without food. It reminded him of the Taoist sages who lived for millennia on air, acorns and their own thoughts.

'Healthy but perilous,' responded Dashlazer.

'How so?'

'A young man like you is not likely to understand the more pressing sort of chaos that life in the rainforest entails.'

'But it seems so peaceful,' said Theo gesturing to the tweeting of birdsong and the crackling fire.

'Now perhaps, but these patches are interrupted with upheavals, storms and disease.'

'Instability,' nodded Theo sagaciously.

'I wouldn't say instability,' he replied.

'I have this friend in America. He is the one I'm working with and he has a theory that there is no stability in the universe. Everything is changing and people who quest for stability whether economic, personal or political are deluded and weak. What do you think of that?'

'The fact that this environment throws up the odd catastrophe does not make it unstable.'

'He seems to think that stability is a kind of death. Instability is synonymous with life and change whilst stability and permanence are symbols of death.'

'The ecosystem depends on both.'

'How?'

'The intertwining of species demands permanence. Look

around. Tiny plants sprout from orchids while vines collide with trees forming braided coils bending into junctions transporting sap and providing walkways for squirrels. Tendrils and liana make monkey ladders and the pale green tubes of cacti dilate for hawk-moth mouths only. This interaction requires time and climatic stability to allow each species to hone in on their evolutionary niche building a foundation for cross-species relations.'

'So where does impermanence come in?' asked Theo.

'The occasional uprooting of the rainforest allows new openings lest there grow any kind of hierarchy or dogma.'

'Yes, he agrees with that. He says cosmic law is omni-polar.'

'So who is this friend?' Ashley asked chewing on some reserpine.

'He is a neuro-alchemist from upstate New York. We have been working together on a project to adjust the recent trajectory of human evolution by collecting a few samples of earth for a hallucinogenic compound.'

'Samples?'

'Yes. We are planning to build a drug that will reignite humanity's spiritual impulse and withdraw us from techno-industrial modernity.'

'I see,' nodded Ashley gravely. 'What do you need?'

'Palm honey, the whistle of a peasant and kava kava.'

'Hmm.'

'Do you think you can help me?'

'Certainly. We can find some palm honey on the Weston Hills. As for the whistle I fear as a Lord I would not qualify.'

'Well, you are in rags now.'

'It depends how rigorous the collection needs to be. If you are doing it to the letter you ought to find a real peasant.'

'It is not that rigorous. In Africa I failed to get hold of parts and took far longer than I was supposed to. This kind of mission demands poetic license. What about kava kava?'

'There's certainly no shortage of that,' Ashley chuckled, walking to a small pot near the terrapin and, pulling out a fibrous fruit, he peeled the skin off and passed it to Theo. 'A warmifier,' he said. Theo put the beige pulp into his mouth.

'Don't swallow it. The fibres are too tough to be digested.

Just keep chewing.' It was hard and bitter. Theo gushed his mouth with saliva to loosen the fibres. After a few minutes it began to moisten and his lips and tongue became numb as the relaxant spread into his cheeks and brain.

The world softened into honesty. Picking up a pebble, he was conscious of each angle, turn of colour, the emptiness versus the precise weight and he tossed it into a small puddle. As it sank, his perception sank into the substance of the earth and from inside every crust of matter emerged a mighty glow. Soon after spotting this pleasure force that pervades objects his heart expanded at the realization that form is nothing because the dynamism of emptiness has the jumble sale universe swirling around a warm centre. After a little head rush he stood up to this realization and looked with fresh eyes at the burgeoning upgrowth and multitudinous animal life that surrounded him including; the red-back salamander, the yellow-bellied flycatcher and the sepia-willied mole. With a casual kick of the foot he overturned a handful of dark soil and decaying skeletal leaves. Aphids, earwigs and wasp feet co-inhabited a T'sang dynasty and he felt an integral joy, untouched by mind-babble; a cloud of amnesia sinking to the core lobe of his being.

He thought of writing a haiku but could not remember the syllabic rules so he ran his finger along the edge of a leaf instead, a kind of 'haiku-in-action'. His consciousness floated in the space of deep time, ambling through the Mesozoic era and the Triassic epoch to recline finally with tree wallabies and Tasmanian wolves. Panthers arched their nigrescent backs in the chaste moonlight, whose fractured beams split into hundreds of creamy splashes through the branches to rest sadly upon the green, rich earth. Ashley gave him a couple of snails and he ate them gladly, while the jungle was filled with mating calls and the old man lay down on the soil and slept.

The moaning of the jungle reminded Theo of the mountainous sexual task that lay ahead and, sobered by the recollection and wide awake after his energizing supper, he decided to leaf through the sex manual before sleep. Chapter Two outlined the stages of the reproductive act, tracking the flow of energy and its manifestation in various forms of mating behaviour.

Nibbling the Golden Flower – How to Know She's Hot for it

Lung – she sighs, with heavy breathing and increased saliva production.

Heart – she reaches out her tongue, pulse quickens.

Spleen and Pancreas – she grips him and pulls him towards her as if taking in food.

Kidney – vaginal dilation, trembling of the thighs and spasmosis of the muscles.

Blood – she bubbles and cannot control herself.

Spirit – she undergoes utter physical collapse and her body unites with oxygen and realm of thought.

The redemption of the species depended on Theo's ability to push a woman into the realm of physical collapse, or 'spirit', and whilst he still fell victim to feelings of inadequacy and fear, the heat of the tropical night had an expanding effect on his mojo and he fell into a deep and confident sleep to the faint but all pervading sound that was somewhere between rustling, shuffling, whispering and crackling.

Ashley gave Theo bits of labour to do the following morning while he scouted around for good sources of palm honey. It was mostly Zen activities such as lifting logs, chopping wood and carrying water. Theo dug a new route for the spring water to travel down and fashioned a bird-table for the condors, but the highlight of his day was the invention of a tool to clear the moss from the gaps in the patio. It allowed him to eject traces of moss from gaps of different widths by lining up indentations for slate sheets of varying thickness. Here is a small sketch.

THE MOSS USURPER

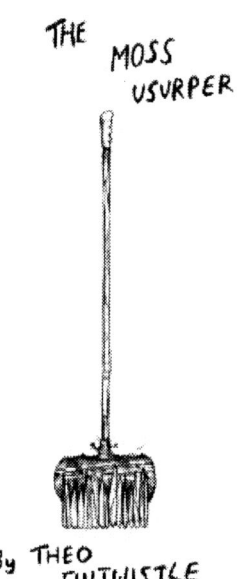

By THEO FINTWISTLE

As the sun reached a central point Ashley collected Theo and took him to the Weston Hills. Hundreds of palm trees hugged the earth and washing lines of spider silk connected them via a pulley system based on a crab shell. Ashley tried to scrape the honey into a clay pot and pass it down to Theo, but the sap from the low lying trees had dried out. To get a scoop they had to climb the higher trees and Theo soon found himself fifteen feet up dangling nervously as heavy pots shot past his head, his balance not helped by the slippery rains that began falling later that afternoon making him drop several pots. When ominous clouds gathered Theo feared another surrender, but after introspecting briefly he reconnected himself to the fundamental bravery of his own soul. In fact, the clapping thunder and first bursts of lightning filled him with Nietzschean ecstasy. The fountains of rain and turbulence of sky converted into kinetic energy rushing up Theo's legs, inspiring him to build new planets and be a rising lover, blood pumping through the arterial system while he soared like a falcon over the world with bass-emanating testicles.

 The mud became slushy and turned into quicksand, and branches began to sway in the wind. Ashley leapt off the tree and grabbed onto a Kauri branch hanging adjacent to him. A small river running along the earth began to bulge and no longer just carried water but live animals too. A million bats flashed out of nowhere while monkeys, koalas and worms scrambled for safety alongside the mightiest tyrants of the jungle fleeing the rains. Numerous trees toppled, their roots tearing up through the soil and falling with a crash as the wrath of God brought out the salty adrenaline of mortality. The palm tree was shaking and as it tilted Theo threw his body towards the Kauri like a Neil Armstrong of the moon of bravery only to slip and come crashing down to earth.

His right leg bent backwards and the pain sent him into delirium. Ashley scampered down and tied Theo to the Kauri trunk with his belt and then jumped over rocks and crags back to his abode. He forced his way through the winds and returned to Theo an hour later with a homemade first aid kit, and when the terror began to calm he administered some pain relieving acupuncture with pine needles. As Theo's body relaxed, Ashley tied a hardy cobra-skin around the damaged knee and fed him a mixture of morphine, badger semen and peyote.

II

The following day the rainforest began to shuffle as sunlight flooded into the gloomy marsh. Hummingbirds took to the sky, frogs helped flies to fix their roofs and while the lions and the sheep weren't exactly laying down with one another, they were certainly getting on better than usual. Theo was in and out of consciousness, and Ashley gave him papaya to dissolve internal mucus and pineapple juice as an anti-inflammatory while performing a bit of invasive surgery.

As Theo stirred he opened his right eye and the world loomed alien and confused. The morphine and peyote twisted his body into green and brown waves of primal angst. Visions burst from the archaic strata of his psyche and projected steamy phantasms onto dead, inert rocks. The world confronted him in a panoply of strange forms, a cinematic labyrinth of xylophonic fission. The universe also seemed to have shrunk by about 800%, making him the size of an acorn and shrubs look like skyscrapers. To cap it all off, French mathematician Henri Poincaré suddenly appeared in front of him in a wizard's gown.

'Bonjour. Ze universe increased in size by 800%. Because you travelled beyond ze speed of light your body vibrates a different frequency.'

'Why has it expanded?' asked Theo.

'Every few months ze universe takes a large inhalation and a few days later exhales, a kind of ontological sigh.'

'What am I supposed to do?'

'You will return to normal size shortly. For food and board there is a nice weevil motel, and here are ze directions,' said Poincaré, handing Theo a small map before disappearing. Theo stood up and felt no pain. He took half an hour to traverse a leaf and though he looked around for Ashley he soon realized that Poincaré had told no lie. Sitting on a rabbit dropping, the impervious demands of the stomach returned. Once again he shouted but most microscopic species ignored him or told him to put a sock in it, so he made his way to the weevil motel. There was a flickering neon sign at the front and a bored-looking grub smoked a cigarette at reception and read a celebrity magazine while a fan turned slow in the heat to the sound of the Elvis classic 'I'm a weevil/my middle name is misery.'

'I'd like to book a room please,' requested Theo. Various insects slurped around, among them some larvae, mites and a young mantis couple annoyingly in love. The receptionist sneered and took out a file.

'Single or double?'

'Single please.'

'How long?'

'Just the night.' said Theo. She asked for his passport. He said he did not have one and that was why he was travelling in the fifth dimension, which caused him to slip through the net of the ontological expansion process. She frowned, gave him a key and told him that dinner would be served at ten. He followed the corridor down to room 35 and entered his depressing room, the pale bed and small bedside table functional. Theo whistled, did some arm exercises and checked his testicles for any lumps. His sense of reality was too lucid for him to be hallucinating, yet this was just not cricket. He felt no sensation of pain in his leg even though he recalled with a shudder the agony racking his body only the day before. Also, he was the size of a little insect. It was a pity the sex manual did not shrink as well since he could not move the project along at this lowly height in any other way.

He took a rain check on dinner to get an early night but unfortunately the mantis couple had rented the room next to Theo's, and soon after he lay down to sleep they began shagging very loudly. He buried his head in the pillow and tried to muffle out the moaning affirmatives, but it was no use. Twenty minutes later they finished in an outcry of ecstasy and sighed in post-coital relief to the sound of the Nora Jones album 'Music to Buy Milk To'.

The calm was shattered by a shriek and Theo leapt out of bed and looked into their room through a grill in the door, fearing some foul play by the male. In fact, the female had extricated herself from their embrace and, spreading her arms widely, sunk her teeth into his abdomen. Although the male yelped and tried to leap upwards she had knotted his legs together, rendering him immobile. Her wings darted out like the velociraptor from Jurassic Park and, paralyzing her mate with terror, she dug her fingernails into his chest and ripped out his thorax and tore him limb from limb, wings, belly and heart. As he lay dismembered she finished him off by squeezing the breath from his mutilated body. Theo tried to kick the door but it was locked so he ran to reception where the grub looked even more bored than before.

'Jesus,' he panted. 'A female mantis is murdering her mate in the room next to mine.' She shrugged and went back to her magazine. 'Did you hear me? There is a murder being committed in the room next to mine!'

'It happens all the time,' she said. 'I can move you to another room if you want.'

'Can't you do something?'

'Not my business,' she said.

'Stupid bitch,' shouted Theo, running outside to see if he could climb the wall and get in through the window. There was no piping but a daffodil ran up the side of the building and touched upon their room on the third floor. He clambered up the stalk and neared the battleground, drawing strength from his soul, but although he tried to recall some of Johnson's taekwondo moves the adrenaline prevented him thinking of anything but the here and now. Once he clambered onto the face of the daffodil he perched on the edge of a petal and watched in horror and resign. With his limbs scattered across the floor in a bloodbath, the dude was dead and his tune sung. It was not worth mounting a rescue attempt since Theo was no longer sure he could take on the bitch, and victory would be for nothing now the poor sod had breathed his last.

'Terrible isn't it?' said a fluffy bumblebee standing behind Theo.

'You can say that again!' he said, turning around. 'Does this go on all the time?'

'Amongst them it does. I always try to warn the gentlemen but they never take heed.'

'I spoke to the receptionist and she was very cold about the whole thing.'

'These motels are shady places. Nothing shocks them anymore. Whatever possessed you to stay in this awful dive?'

'Lack of options. I'm stuck at this size until the universe shrinks again.'

'Until it what?'

'Never mind.'

'I'm sure I could find you a room at the colony,' said the kind bee. 'I hate to see anybody stay around here.'

'Really?' asked Theo. 'That would be very kind.'

'Hop on,' said the bee. With no luggage or passport Theo jumped on his back and they zoomed through the bushes and shrubs. Two minutes later the bee screeched to a halt next to a slit door in the hollow trunk of a dead tree.

'Password?' came a voice from the other side.

'Gold plate,' said the bee and the door opened. As they walked through a pollen detector, two bees in combat gear pounced on Theo, poking him with their antennae and sniffing. The philosopher cried for help and the bee who invited him pulled off the guards with a laugh.

'Okay,' he said. 'He's with me.'

'What is he, Doc?' asked one of the guards. 'He looks like a tiny hairless bear!'

'He is a roaming traveller who just needs a place to sleep.'

After some persuasion the guard bee let Theo into the hive and, passing the second level of gates, he overlooked the splendid factory. Scores of bees laboured in a synchronized system, a maze of tunnels and crevices forming an orgiastic drone and a cooperative productivity to make Karl Marx catch his breath. Two grand chandeliers hung in the mess hall where they dined, as well as a poster of a beautiful young bee reaching down her skirt to retrieve a tennis ball. In the female camp there was a poster of a bee who looked not dissimilar to Arnold Schwarzenegger wearing a leather jacket and a pair of sunglasses, entitled 'The Pollinator'.

Because it was nighttime the temperature was dropping so a crew of workers walked around giving off body heat with a rapid flexing of their thoracic flight muscles. Others would hug together in groups of ten while one bee flapped his wings and pushed the warm air from within their brotherly scrum to the rest of the hive. Tired and bemused, Theo said he was weary. Doc Bee showed him to his room and told him that breakfast would be served at six. Theo looked around his room and was impressed. The cells were functional but also aesthetic because the hexagonal structure of the rooms made maximum use of minimum space meaning that one bee's ceiling is another one's floor, which is great as long as the bee below doesn't listen to Linkin Park.

Theo thanked him for his kindness, immediately fell asleep and began dreaming. (Although the way things were going he no longer drew sharp distinctions between dreams and reality. He had not really seen reality since Christmas and the colour of his life had become varying shades of the baffling.)

Refreshed and sprightly the next morning, he was introduced to the population. The male bees were plump and hairy with large eyes and a droning sound, whilst the worker bees, who removed waste and buried the dead, were small, furry and female. The division of labour was spread according to age. The young bees would clean and dust the cells, while the four-week-olds would do the fanning and tend to the whims of the Queen. Ten-week-olds collected pollen and the 20-week-olds secreted the beeswax. The ailing 22-week-olds did the accounts and 34-week-olds bored everybody stiff with stories about the war.

There was a real buzz about the place that day because a

number of young bees were making their first orientation flight in which they leap into the world, circle around a bit and then come back. A whole queue of them lined up outside Doc Bee's room smoking cigarettes, acting cool and wearing their baseball caps backwards. Although claiming they had to see him for duty, they really wanted him to calm their fears. Some showed him their technique and asked if it was up to scratch while others asked him to recount stories of his first flight. Patiently and paternally, he answered their questions and mollified their fears whilst knowing that among them there might be one who would either get lost, expend too much vital energy early on and collapse or else become entangled in a flower, bush or shrub. The bell rang throughout the hive and everyone gathered by a specially made platform near the front door, which had flags up and a table with various trophies. The youngsters stood nervously at the launch pad, their goggles and swim caps fastened stretching their legs and doing breathing exercises.

'It's great that you get to see this,' said Doc Bee. 'It's quite a moment.' The whistle blew and they lifted into the air, while the older bees took a coffee break and sat around enjoying a few moments of rest. Their eyes became dewy as they thought back to their beautiful youths all those weeks ago, and Theo listened in to the amusing stories and the melancholy as they recalled the bees that never made it. Minutes later the fledgling bees started returning, their tufty hair windswept and their limbs shaking with exhaustion. Some attempted to impress the female workers with a diving loop-the-loop at the end, which mostly ended with a head-butt against the front wall. Brief though it was, the orientation flight was their first taste of adult struggle.

A wailing siren screamed into the air, which Theo assumed was a celebratory toot until he saw everyone leap from their chairs and run for safety. They hid under tables, hugged together and ran in circles looking for their loved ones. Many dashed towards the front door and tried to lock it shut with bolts made out of twigs and beeswax, leaning their backs against it and covering every nook and cranny. A curious yellow gas seeped in and made them delirious, falling over and vomiting while tears streamed out of their eyes and they writhed on the floor. The front door was kicked down and a gang of bees on motorbikes with bandannas and tattoos entered with half-smoked cigarettes dangling from their mouths. Theo groaned, for he felt as though odd events were lining up like penguins to jump into the sea of his life. The gang kicked aside any bees that were not immobilized and headed towards the storage cells. With hammers and axes they broke through the security, filled their sacks with honey and turned to leave. As they departed from the hive, the leader took out his cigarette end and spat it onto the floor, scrunching it against the carpet with his foot.

Bees came around very gradually, rubbing their heads and feeling woozy. Once they had regained composure and balance they trudged around the colony fixing the damage.

'What the hell was that?' Theo asked Doc Bee.

'I forgot to tell you,' he sighed. 'They are robber bees. They make their living by emitting a substance called citral, which is a poisonous lemony gas. It jams up our nasal passages, disturbs the sensory system and renders us defunct. Then they march in, steel our booty, pillage the place and move on to the next hive.'

'That is awful. How often do they do this?'

'Once every few days.'

'Do you lose everything?'

'About fifty per cent of our labour output,' he nodded. 'If it wasn't for them we would not have to work so hard. It becomes a real strain.'

'Can't you do something? Are there any police around?'

'They are different species of bee. Our police would not be able to do anything. Besides, they don't rob us for leisure. It is their evolutionary job.'

'Doing a job is one thing, but smashing up the place is quite another. Have you thought about any defensive measures?'

'We have tried so many but none of them seem to work. We filled the door with amber sap but that means no one can leave or come in so we lose the same labour. We have hidden the storage honey, but they always sniff it out.'

'How does the gas work?'

'It functions when it passes through our mouths. It begins to work, travelling through our bodies and moving to our wings. If we could stop it entering our bodies we would be fine.'

'Have you thought about gas masks?'

'What?'

'Gas masks.'

'What are they?'

'You know, gas masks. Masks that stop you inhaling gas.'

'I don't understand the words.'

'What, gas mask?'

'Yes. I've never heard of that before.'

'You must've heard of it!'

'What is it?'

'It is a mask that you wear to stop breathing gas.'

'What's breathing?'

'You've never heard of breathing?'

'No.'

'Look,' said Theo starting to explain. 'A gas mask is a patch...'

'Are you feeling okay?' asked Doc Bee.

'What do you mean, am I feeling okay?'

'You aren't making much sense. You keep coming out with bizarre words.'

'Patch?'

'I think you should lie down.'

'Do you have a dictionary here?'

'Of course.'

'Please fetch it for me.'

'Fine, but you will not find those words in there.'

Doc Bee brought the dictionary from the hive library and left Theo in the reading room while the other bees gathered themselves. The book was exhaustive, with every word you would find in the most comprehensive English dictionary. Words like mendacious. Yet when Theo reached the place where you would expect to find the words gas, mask, patch, elastic, inhalation or prevent he was met with a curious gap. The text would skip from an earlier word to a later one.

> **Pat** *verb 1. To touch or stroke lightly, especially with an open hand.*
> **Patchouli** *noun 1. The oil of an Asian plant used in perfume.*

Gas was the same.

> **Garter** *noun 1. A band worn around the leg to keep a sock in place.*
> **Gash** *noun 1. A long deep wound, especially in the flesh.*

He soon realized that this was not an unfortunate coincidence, and nor was it a case of lazy editorship. It was a necessity; nature. Since the conflict between these two bees was not a grudge but an evolutionary dynamic, their relationship depended upon prerequisites, and in order for both species to survive, nature built in certain faults to the victims. Anything connected with gas or being gassed was never in their cognitive library in the first place, and the limits of their reality was defined by their genetic wiring. Theo explained this to Doc Bee and asked for some materials. They brought him whatever scraps they could find and left him there, convinced that the citral had interfered with his cognitive function. He sifted through the twigs, shavings and crusts extracting tiny fibres to act as elastic and formed a prototype gas mask.

'Ingenious!' cried Doc when Theo called him in shortly afterwards. 'That way, we stop the stuff moving in. We will be protected!'

'Exactly,' said Theo. 'Now get a load of the same materials, call in some worker bees and I'll show them how to build it.' At first the worker bees were sceptical, but Theo demonstrated how it worked. A sector of the back left chamber was cordoned off and desks were hauled in while a number of bees were hand-picked and got down to work.

Ready and armed, the hive had great faith in this foreign stranger and could hardly wait for the next invasion. Two days passed, with Theo becoming evermore angsty about his own project, particularly as the cobra skin no longer seemed to be strapped to his mysteriously healed leg. Lack of internet resources or telephones meant he could make no contact with

Spinny, who would probably want news on progress. He paced around waiting for the ontological shrink, but the wailing sirens came first. The bees did not try bolting the door, and everyone strapped their masks on as the citral came through the gaps. The burglars kicked down the door with their cowboy yee-haas expecting the booty but were met instead with an army of mean-ass motherfuckers standing in a daunting stillness. Doc Bee stepped forward and tapped a baseball bat against his open palm and the burglars froze in their tracks. Doc spat out his chewing gum and said, 'Who's your Daddy? Who's your Daddy now, punks?'

III

'Theo!' came Ashley's voice, working through the maze of disembodied confusion and bringing the philosopher back to earth. The Englishman opened his eyes and felt great pain in his leg. He looked down and saw the cobra skin still strapped to him and the texture of the world had lost those trimmings of fantasy which adorned the micro-reality of recent days. 'I had to get you back conscious again,' said Ashley, stirring up a drink of some sort. 'While you were out cold I tried to whistle but couldn't manage it. I've never done it before and I had a cleft lip as a child so I think it's impossible.' Theo nodded and adapted himself back to this world. 'I went to see the Buddhists on the other end of the island and asked if they could whistle. They said they would like to help you but they're about to commence a silent retreat, so if you want them to whistle for you then you had better head over there soon. I wanted you to enter a deep Navajo healing trance but this news forced me to awaken you with bromeline. How are you planning to collect the whistle?'

'I, er, yes. I have a small vial and they have to whistle into the vial. Sorry Ashley, I'm a bit dazed. What the boggle is going on?'

'I fed you a mixture to summon your natural powers and this sends you into a powerful visionary underworld. There is normally a smooth transition back to this plane but I suspected you couldn't wait until their retreat was over.'

'No, fine. Thank you. It was a good decision, I just need to gather myself. When do they commence this retreat?'

'Tomorrow,' he said. 'If you feel up to it I think you should head over there this evening. Or if you'd rather you can give me the vial and I'll go.'

'That's very kind,' said Theo. 'But I really ought to go. I've made such a mess of this project so far and I need to take control. Besides, I'm interested in those guys and I'd like to meet them.'

'How is the leg?'

'Aches certainly,' said Theo, moving it around a little. 'I'm fairly sure I can walk if it is not too far.'

'It's about 45 minutes through that valley and past the teal lagoon.'

Theo stumbled upright and stretched the wounded limb. He had no idea how long he'd been unconscious but his knee seemed to have made a remarkable recovery. The bees and the weevils he could no longer be sure of. Without further ado and relieved that the project was back in motion he packed his things into *The Beagle* and had a bite to eat with Ashley. Thanking him, they embraced and wished good fortune on each other's shoulders.

After two journeys and one storm, *The Beagle* was looking shaky and Theo took care to move it over even soft ground. He headed towards the teal lagoon, his leg gaining strength as he walked. The pain was dull, constant but tolerable and he was feeling much better for the exercise, and as soon as he passed the lagoon he saw the twinkling lights of the ashram. Of the various monks living there, all of whom he could safely classify as peasants, one would surely be able to whistle and what's more he would like to learn more of their existential system after Spinny spoke in such glowing terms about meditation.

The ashram was simple, sturdy and elegant. Its gardens were immaculately maintained and small bedrooms lay side by side in a pentagon shape around a pagoda. Theo knocked on a number of doors and one monk was present, resting on his bed. He stood up and smiled at Theo.

'Hello there. I was lodging with Ashley, you know Ashley? I

need a whistling noise and he told me he had spoken to you people about it.' The monk looked confused and, raising his finger into the air, walked out of his room and towards the meditation hall. Theo stood outside, clearing some of the rust from the chassis. Some minutes later an elder named Tenzin stepped out of the hall and walked shakily towards him.

'We speak with Ashley,' he said softly. 'I understand you need a whistle noise from peasant?'

'Exactly,' said Theo. 'And as penniless monks without cleft lips I can hardly think of anybody more perfect than you people. Would one of you oblige?'

'I think so,' said the elder. 'Do you want us just whistle?'

'I need one person to whistle into a small glass vial and then seal the vial while the whistle is inside.'

'And that is all?'

'Yes.'

'Fine.' He whistled into the vial and Theo sealed it. There was an awkward feeling, for it was a strange transaction. Theo did not want to turn and depart just like that, so he inquired a little about meditation, for whilst Spinny had referred to it as the greatest door-opener to the dynamics of the subconscious, he never explained what the thing was or how it worked.

'So you people meditate here do you?'

'Yes,' he said quietly and smiling.

'And what is that exactly?'

'Bringing the mind down to point.'

'What for?'

'See perfect.'

'It must require quite a bit of patience,' said Theo admiringly.

'Would you like to try?'

'Well, I am interested to experience it. I've heard great stuff about it but I don't know exactly what it involves. Maybe I could have a lesson?'

'Certainly. We start retreat tomorrow if you want to join.'

'I'm not sure about the retreat,' said Theo doubtfully. 'That sounds quite heavy. Perhaps I could just do an hour or so this evening?'

'Why not try retreat?' he asked encouragingly.

'Well, I don't know if I'd be up to it. I mean I've never done this stuff before.'

'Beginner best. Give it some effort.' He had four weeks left, and he anticipated Barcelona as being the easiest place so far as a result of its shops, markets and people. By far the most societal and developed destination, he was confident he could breeze in and out in around ten days.

'Well, I'll stay tomorrow. My leg still needs a bit of time to recover anyway. Is that okay?'

'Of course. Perhaps you help with some work and cleaning but we want you to meditate with us.' Tenzin took Theo to a spare room and Theo tied *The Beagle* up outside. The silent retreat would commence at dawn.

The gong went at four a.m. the following morning. Tenzin handed Theo some saffron robes and he stumbled bleary-eyed to the meditation hall. Twenty monks and nuns sat motionless on burgundy cushions. Tenzin showed Theo to his cushion at the back and he sat cross-legged, intrigued despite tiredness. When everybody was seated Tenzin took his place at the front and gave foreign instructions. When he finished he looked at Theo and said, 'Feel the movement of breath in and out of your nose.'

'Is that it?' The elder smiled via his cosmo eyes, a twinkle craftiness showing that he had dissolved the crude mass of his mind into ether so fine that gravity could no longer exert an influence.

'Yes. Pay attention to the breath moving in and out of the nose. Thoughts will wander but bring them back to feeling of breath,' and then he closed his eyes. Theo was slightly disappointed with the prosaic instructions, hoping for cosmic visualizations, dramatic tectonic changes into wisdom and the stunning beatitude of enlightenment. Nevertheless, a thousand-mile journey starts with the first step, or the thought of it to be precise.

Every five or six seconds Theo's thoughts flew off to the world of women, triumph and death. He would experience his own thoughts and thus be aware of himself being aware of himself but only occasionally would he be aware of himself experiencing his own thoughts, and at these instants he would return to the feeling of breath through the nostrils. By lunchtime he had been in control of his mind at three instances for about two or three seconds each time. The elder requested he come to the front after the rice and vegetables. He first enquired how Theo felt the meditation had gone and he replied, not very well, and asked what the point was in following the breath through the nostrils. The elder explained to him the basics of Buddhist psychology.

Consciousness is separate from mental contents, he said, and reacts to thoughts and inner states with either craving or aversion. If the thought is negative, self-depreciating or painful, the mind reacts against it either by repressing the danger, transferring the problem onto other people or reaching for the bottle. If the thought is vain, arrogant or self-important the mind craves more of the same. Each time the mind reacts to what it perceives to be positive or negative inner thoughts and emotions, it develops ingrained aversion and craving, which reifies the distinction between pleasure and pain rather than melting them both. In meditation, one consciously avoids reacting to thoughts and as a consequence the accumulated layers of aversion and craving bubble up to the surface and when they too are ignored they pass forever leaving one feeling generally more nimble. By focusing on the breath one begins to dig up the soil of the soul and reveal the hidden demons and dreams which hold the strings of surface consciousness which is their puppet.

Theo returned to his cushion seized with inspiration. His meditation deepened, his breathing became calm and dopamine flowed. Like kumkwats in the summertime, his testicles drooped and his mind attained luminosity. It was as though the electricity of his primal, reptilian brain base passed through some semi-porous membrane and became subjectively intelligible as cosmic unity. The deep heat of the subconscious towered over the stale world of conscious logic whose role is to wash dishes, lick stamps and pair up socks but not to build the world. The mind of the everyday humdrum is a brittle fragment compared to the bio-electric jacuzzi of the mystic soul, and Theo peaked into the Eastern sauna and dug it big style.

He had only been enlightened for a couple of seconds when he was suddenly consumed by aggression and chaotic error, and had his thought patterns knotted uncomfortably. Fidgeting, flashes of red lights and the deconstruction of his self broke up the veneer of sanity to release pent-up sweat, rage and depression. Equanimity went out the window, his heart thumped in blind existential panic for the sorrowful world and the broken future, the unrelenting awareness of incompletion tearing one from the womb of animal comfort. He opened his eyes with a gasp and was surrounded by peaceful shaved heads. He ran out of the pagoda and into the open air wondering whether perhaps the poor ventilation was making his soul unsteady, yet as he walked around the gardens the same curious agitation seized his body. Bloated with the hedonistic pleasures of psychedelia and stifled by the pious constraints of asceticism, Theo concluded that the only redemption for a young man is to lay his cheek upon the soft seat of the female belly. The odds are stacked up for psychosis as an overactive noggin' tries to impress order upon riddles. The bookies are on insanity and collapse, peace of mind is the one-legged horse.

Tenzin approached him and asked if everything was okay. Theo said he was unnerved by the depth of his inner mess and was considering bailing out and applying for a job in media sales. Tenzin took him to the dormitories and gave him a book of the Buddha's thought, returning to the meditation hall and letting Theo off the afternoon session. The philosopher lay down and opened the book and the first page began 'be disgusted at your existence'. Theo closed the book and looked at the ceiling, wondering how far he should persevere with this boat-rocking philosophy, but it loomed like a Pandora's box and he read on. Buddha claimed the universe is an arrow sticking in your eye and there is no happiness to be found in the pleasures of the earth. Man runs wild and his carnal pleasures are ham sandwiched between the bread of pain, yet escape is futile since the very structure of existence is inherent misery and for as long as we look outwards for redemption we are nailed to sorrow. The only revolution is from the mundane mind to the awakened one, to sink to the base of our inner blackness and conquer the universe.

There was spikiness to the lamentations of Buddha, like an inescapable seizure that fixates the mind into a sealed autointoxication. It had something so devastating. The works of philosophers fill a billion dusty libraries, packed with a thousand contentions, critiques and counter responses yet Buddha cut to the raw chase.

> A fault of vision, a mock show
> A dream, a bubble and a cloud
> So should one view the
> Ignorance of conditioned thought

Flushes of pleasure, fame and glory are connected to brain tumours, heartache and war. The heads of pleasure spin with the tails of misery in a unit, a coin-shaped double helix railing to infinity. The sword of Buddha's logic, on the other hand, slew sex and separation, conquest and failure. Dionysian music and perky bosoms were cast to the wind to flutter and decompose with the twin reflection: tragedy and decrepitude. The Shakespearean tapestry of life burns in the fire of meditation leaving the glow of nothingness, wu-wei and emptiness without form.

'But what about grabbing a handful of arse?' Theo wondered. 'What about fat red apples and strong black coffee? And those long psychedelic evenings of multidimensional wonder hazed in smoky mystery and adventures among friends in a hot box van laden with sadness and the promise of orgies twinkling in the discotheque distance?' This austere pessimism ran against the romantic whoosh of mischief and sorrow that only recently splashed into Theo's previously monochrome soul. Yet note this. What lies beyond polarity? We know the score of this up-and-down life. The Harley-Davidson of the soul consumes the chi-petrol to push us through the contours of pleasure and pain until empty, while the landscape remains. As the eyes close to the mountains and fjords of Experience, the internal engine remains packed with force, revving occasionally and hinting at vast amounts of reserve power that nourishes itself and amplifies instead of throwing its energies to the amnesiac sponge of the universe.

'Nature is no butterfly,' Theo thought, and he was right. She will slip arsenic in a man's porridge as soon as he has unleashed his pearly genetic blueprint into the womb of a waffle waitress only so she can give birth to another poor sod. The poor sod will also be forced to trek across the inhospitable earth and choke on his own angst while his father trudges towards stiffness and death only to get reincarnated back into the freezing night, to be gnashed at by bats for millions of years. 'I see you, builder', claimed Buddha on the next page, 'and you shall build no more house for me for I have destroyed your materials. I have smelted the wheel of samsara with the laser of meditation and struggled free from the selfish monkey ego of genes into the cool meta-animal light.' Theo mused on Buddha's achievement. How he stubbornly sat – to sit – sitting – which contravenes all the nauseating forces that yank one like a tin raft in a storm. Nietzsche stood up to the fierce whips and scorns and said, 'Again! Hit me again!' and claimed that life-denying religions were for the weary and the defeated, yet Buddha made a toy out of the world that crippled Nietzsche. Theo closed the book and said, 'The Lord of the universe is Buddha's brain. All other men should be measured only by their proximity to him like small moons circling Jupiter.'

The project beckoned, and though he had barely made it past the first day of the retreat Theo felt he had grasped the essence of Buddhism and its genius was undoubted – a hasty conclusion having only practised it for four hours, but it confronted him with the obviousness of the blue sky. Theo spoke to Tenzin, who was disappointed he was leaving so soon but glad for his enthusiasm, and they parted ways. Theo packed himself into *The Beagle* and moved into an open space away from the ashram. 'To Barcelona!' he cried pulling the lever, and the pod zoomed into the sunset with a nuclear flash of the heart and the four wheels of dharma spinning mad and forever.

Barcelona
Graffiti, Jugglers

I

After the heart-stretch of Africa and the existential puzzle of Viti Levu, Theo felt relieved to be heading somewhere as cosmopolitan as Barcelona. It was high time he enjoyed a boogie, for whilst the human spirit had been revealed in its red warmth and the Buddha had emerged as the cure for strife, what Theo now required was girls and action. He suffered the bumpiest landing so far, the underside of *The Beagle* trembling with rust and structural weakness as the parachute burst very late and got tangled up on the black gates around Park de la Ciudadella. The canopy required a fair bit of pushing and shoving to open and Theo had to cut the pod loose with his penknife to lower the vehicle safely to the ground. The park in darkness was perfect, allowing him to avoid the attention and mania of the busy streets. Nervous about the pod being stolen, Theo slept in the cockpit.

He awoke late the following afternoon filled with a desire for carnal power to realign the yin passivity of the retreat. He carefully disguised the pod beneath a periwinkle bush and marched into the city, the sunshine and thrum inspiring an outburst of animal vitality. He entered a glitzy restaurant and ordered two rump steaks and a bottle of wine. 'Never mind Gandhi!' he said to the Moroccan waiter. 'He couldn't even walk ten yards without getting cramp in his calves. I want to be a warrior!' He let out a loud roar which attracted the attention of everyone in the restaurant and some pedestrians. The steak came and he devoured the offal and blood, gorging himself upon its sinews and ripping its flesh with his canines, drinking the wine and smoking a fat reefer from the dregs of his

Ghanaian weed until being asked to leave by the hotelier and stumbling into De Guispucoa Rambla.

He bounced through the streets revelling in the excitement of his monastic release and heavy with the dull ache of testicular plenitude yearning for release. His vegetarian austerity had heightened his senses and as the sun fell and a navy influence hit the alleyways he veered into the red-light district along the cobbled roads and approached a peep show building. The bar-woman, an old haggard rat-face of a disappointed old bag, looked at him and said nothing, pressing her lips together so that small cat-like wrinkles emerged through her moustache.

'I'd like to see a naked woman,' he announced.

'Show?' she answered.

'Er, I don't know. Is that how things are done? I mean, I've never—'

'Speak English?'

'Yes.' Theo squirmed. Two men sitting by the scarlet window chuckled into their tall drinks and both had smoky faces made grey by bad fortune. She pointed at a black cubicle and handed Theo change in exchange for his notes. His stomach was dancing the funky chicken, his hands were trembling faster than a bee's wing-flap and his balls ululated like two deep-sea jellyfish in the throes of love.

He closed the door and waited in the pitch black room. 'Is she going to come in here?' he wondered. 'Am I to wait? There's no room to do anything in this telephone booth!' He looked at the fetid spunk capsule, imagining its history; dirty frustrated gloopy-eyed old chicken-fat men pumping their spinal fluid against the blackened wall, beer-smeared pores and drunken bastards and nervous but bravado tearaways. After three minutes he noticed a small coin-receiving slit and giggled at the oneness. The coin rattled in and a light revealed a girl in a bedroom behind a Perspex screen. She was clad in her underwear, writhing about on a bed and touching herself in all the regions of interest to a young man dedicated to the pursuit of religious enhancement, but soon after she found her groove the light turned off.

'Hey!' he shouted, banging on the window, 'You call that a

peep show! That's a disgrace! I didn't even peep a peep of a peep!' He put another coin in, and she resumed, each time revealing a little more, sometimes arching back and sliding the fabric to one side and showing her entire mystery. (Although it was not really a mystery as Theo saw up close, just a conglomeration of valves, keyholes and doorways... oh, and the ancient cave encapsulating the elusive button-jewel – little time to make the strike, a few seconds perhaps. Like Medusa, she mustn't know you're looking.) Theo soon realized something was awhiff. She was making signals to him implying that the peep was to entice, an aperitif to be followed by the fish and chips enterprise of fucking, but he could nay afford it, and besides he was here on business – the business of gathering the tones of the techni-world – and he ought to save his seed for a more mythic female.

He left the building and approached people to start conversations in case they could help but they all walked away quickly. How he wished there was a way of opening up his chest and showing his pure, red heart! Although when the light of day became inky he felt excited with the lack of order, he had loitered in Ghana and the Pacific, meaning time was of the essence so he hurried back to the park and scrolled through his notes in the pod. Under the title of Barcelona Spinny mentioned a man called Patrick Wright, a journalist who had once done an article on Spinny as part of a counter-culture piece for a magazine. Theo took the paper to the tourist information booth and the man frowned trying to make out the illegible handwriting and, giving up, gave Theo a map of Barcelona. Theo tracked down the road on the map and hopped on the Metro standing up and holding the dangly as it rumbled through the underground. He made occasional eye contact with someone sitting down but they were stuck in the awkward social gamble. Neither of them wanted to go 😊 in case the other went 🙁 but neither of them wanted to go 🙁 in case the other went 😊 So in the end, they both went 😐

On arrival Theo spent fifteen minutes trying to figure out which was right and left and after a further hour of wandering around asking people and being shooed away he found the apartment block. He pressed the buzzer for Flat Three. Silence.

166

He buzzed again and there was a clicking, breaking noise and a voice – female.

'Ola?'

'Ah, ola, yes. Do you speak English?'

'Yes.'

'Are you? No, of course you're not. What I mean is, I'm looking for Patrick Wright. I'm a friend of Spinny. Patrick once did an article about him.'

'What you want?'

'I need some help. I'm here on an expedition to gather the last few ingredients for a psychoactive drug that will reconnect human consciousness to the biosphere.' There was a pause.

'Patrick's not here at the moment.'

'Where is he?'

'He's in a meeting on the main square.'

'Whereabouts?' There was another pause. 'Look, I know this all sounds a bit ludicrous but I really am a friendly and nice guy. I'm small and not violent. I just need to speak to him.'

'He is at a restaurant called Dariare, opposite the Gaudi Museum.'

'What does he look like?' She paused. 'Never mind. I'll find him myself,' said Theo and he made his way quickly to the restaurant. He scoured around, but no one called Patrick was present. Theo was asked to leave by the owner because he was annoying the clients and he complied, nabbing a cheap bottle of wine on his way out. He sozzled up and the increase in sensory feeling perked a desire to play arcades in the meantime. He quested around for a parlour, finally settling into the neon glow pixels of Daytona. At one point, whilst negotiating a tricky corner and trying to overtake two of his enemies, a handsome dark Spanish lad in a white vest and cheap jeans stood behind resting his arm like James Dean on the side of the car with a cigarette smouldering between his fingers. Theo stepped up his driving skills only to tumble head over heels and return to last position. The lad grinned and blew out smoke.

'Mas rapido!'

'Sorry?' said Theo. Alfonso rolled his eyes and grabbed the wheel, overtaking the enemy on the outside, and gave the wheel back to Theo. Theo thanked him and moved up to thirteenth but then crashed back to last place.

'Du es Ingles, English? Eh?' said the fellow, the mahogany of his skin glistening with sweat from the lights. 'Tu hugar commo cacha. You play it like shit!' Theo laughed. 'You try always on the inside, wrong, they crush... Outside, slow, tranquiolo,' he motioned with his hands, 'slower but then win!' He pumped his coins in. He was about to nab in past the front man at the last bend, and he called out to his friends to witness the victory and they walked over in smoke and smiles with eyes red and slow. Quavier was of medium height saying little but giggling occasionally, Montpellier was darty and winky while Luc was sinuous and muscular, with black-brown eyes and broad shoulders; a rabble of shifty unkempt youths; cheeky and harmless criminals, arrogant and spunky, in denim with moon-white vests dangling from their hips.

They wandered the streets whispering romantic poetry to the olive-legged princesses who strode beneath the warm lights and sat in cafeterias drinking coffee and pouting. Aye, to watch with eyes of rushing criminality painted on the backdrop of pleasure in the feast of life and women; ripe squidgy avocados and opulent hashish resin, upper body strength and deft footballing trickery. Straightaway they zoomed out pulling him along like a rubber ring behind a motorboat, munching oranges and yakking like fools in the zest of the Barcelona roads teeming with graffiti artists and jugglers. Theo's presence seemed to spark a little light into that day, for beneath all their mischief was a kind of hopeless boredom, and the intrepid Englishman gave the minors an excuse to roam over their favourite corners of the town. Theo was glad to be so readily taken up, hoping that these would be his guiding angels to lead him to the treasure, yet he soon remembered *The Beagle.*

'Eh, Alfonso.'

'Yes?'

'I wonder if you could help me. I have some luggage that I need storing, somewhere safe.'

'Suitcase?'

'Not exactly. A vehicle. We have to find somewhere for it.'

'Where is it, then, now?'

'Behind a periwinkle bush in the park.'

'Okay,' smiled Alfonso. 'I know a place.' Alfonso agreed to meet his friends shortly and Theo took him to the park to reveal the unsteady-looking pod. Alfonso frowned and took Theo back to his bed-sit in the red-light district. Inside hung a fishing line, busted cans of petrol, shards of metal, crisps, dirty clothing and hundreds of broken watches. They put *The Beagle* up against the wall and went to catch up with Montpellier and Luc on the beach, where there were bonfires, giggling girls, boasting boys and night-time. Thump-wah-woo music blared as hundreds of youths ran into the water in bikinis and shorts with breasts and torsos blazing while splashing the salty surf around in arcs of black-blue. Theo was tossed into the sea where his nasal tubes filled with water. He swam out to a rock and scaled its peak, to look back upon the dancing and reach out into the space-empathy for the single form that had fragmented itself into shards of people; it now glued back into oneness and the separated limbs and hearts stuck inwardly with seaweed.

Theo returned to shore, smoked to the bottom of his lungs, swigged wine and ate his way through a ketchup soaked hotdog. The youths laughed at the Englishman, introducing him to their friends. Theo shook their hands and said hello and smiled and they asked him questions, but he was too hammered and jiving with eagerness at the bonfire until he was introduced to Lioba, a turquoise temptress with cotton thighs, pert eyes and a twinkling stud pierced through her tanned belly. Her eyes were brown coconut, lavished with a streak of volcanic green around big, open pupils. Across her torso lay a tattered rope cream top with holes and underneath that a black T-shirt and beneath that justice a soft tumbling heaven passed her navel into the shuttle of love. Her body glowed with the bonfiery moonlight of all ever and the milky astronomo-beams fell in a silent way upon the soft of her thigh – and as for her behind, it relegated the transfiguration of Christ to a grey cloud. It made the Big Bang look like the sigh of an old man. Ah, the female buttocks, sending bricklayers and lawyers alike into knee-wobbling paeans of delirium with a simple shimmy.

It seemed strange to Theo, evolutionarily speaking, for buttocks to be so profoundly sexy given that their function is that of a poo-emitter, a seat and an appropriate conclusion to the business of legs. Nevertheless, hers were a treasure.

Theo could barely stand up straight, singing and jumping up and down with his trousers unbuttoned and hair skew-whiff shouting, 'Tics of gear and franzines! Tubs of industrial glue from late-night punks in the ark, the mad skateboarders and squatters and dropouts and rascalanian zeelines from the undone jilt. Liquid ivory splattered across the screen of existence in the great getaway, jeestomping into the field in the freeze-frame night!' Although it was not computer manual syntax he communicated his feelings clearly. The evening rattled on like a cheap but sturdy prank van along dusty roads headed for sleep as the party dwindled, the dancing subsided with a sad poof! and everyone returned to their abodes like stray and ragged things.

As soon as the sun arrived for work Theo began to feel nauseous. It had been a reckless few days; a big steak and a bottle of wine, a peep show, bouncing stoned through the sweaty streets into an arcade parlour, rushing around with a load of strangers and smoking cheap hashish in the bustle of a Continental night, another two bottles of wine at the bonfire party with hotdogs and chocolate truffles and crisps and skinny-dipping and rolling around in the sand, topped off with jumping up and down and spinning around nonstop for ten minutes. Never mind the Young Hegelians. The only revolution Theo could contemplate now was the one in his abdomen, and he began vomiting gallons of tacky wine and food heaving forth onto the corner of the street in a pitter-patter of half-digested, orange-red matter. Alfonzo was sympathetic, and he shooed away the interested pedestrians while Theo wretched with his forehead glistening sweaty. He tried to gain leverage over his sickness by thinking of the sun; its steadiness.

Theo rested the next day, savouring his breaths, his quiet stomach and the soothing motions of the streets. The world returned to wellness as he stood by the window like Albert Camus and watched the motion from a distance, laying down and stroking his seven chest hairs and sticking to humble foods; dry toast with dairylea, plain pasta and unsweetened semolina. Alfonso nursed him back to health with some milk of magnesia and some of the coal dust from the bonfire had stuck to his trousers, two of the elements he needed from this leg of the journey.

'Eh, ge tal?'
'Better. Thank you.'
'Tranquilo. Rest. You stay with us till better. If you want you can stay.'
'Yes yes, I would.'

II

Theo returned to activity the next day and docked with them, waltzing around town as if he owned the gaff. Some nights he, Alfonso and Luca would pace in the blue lights of the pavement, running up old buildings or sitting opposite one another with their backs against cracked walls throwing a forlorn tennis ball to and fro, perhaps to remove their outer garments and keel into sleep and open their somnolent eyes in the morning to the muttering and confused pointing and whispers of concerned and well-meaning Japanese tourists. At other times Theo would stay in the bedsit and practice Taoist sex techniques, his perineum muscle starting to flex notably. Alfonso came and went, spoke little but had a basic goodness and respect for Theo and was happy for the Englishman to crash on his sofa.

On the Friday, running dangerously close to firefly termination, Alfonso and his pals were due to play their weekly football match in an old tenement building near the market. Theo stopped into an internet café that afternoon to work through his overflowing in-box. He had several hundred emails, many pornographic or marketing circulars, but some from Cambridge telling him that a ceasefire had been called and the university was running regularly again which meant, of course, they were expecting his dissertation in one week. Chummy sent a particularly acidic note telling him that if he did not return at once he would fail his degree. It would have been unthinkable a year previously, but it had now become a possibility. He paced back immediately and opened his portmanteau but whilst he had made notes and jottings here and there over the recent weeks he had nothing anywhere near approaching a cogent thesis and he was overtaken with despair which manifested in a terrible state of lounging around.

He gazed out of the window for a couple of hours, almost made a cup of tea, seriously considered a few ideas and rubbed his cheek against the sofa. He then threw a pencil up and caught it for half an hour followed by a long stint of lying down and watching the slow opium drifting of those anonymous tufts of airborne square feathers. He consoled himself of any guilt by remembering that an obsession with academic brilliance is a sign of subconscious tension and the anal need for pure excellence is an ego compensation for the shit-stained walls of the subconscious. Whilst this was a novel excuse for laziness, it might cause a dangerous inactivity that could spread to the project which, despite a leap and jump, still held challenges and difficulties and smallness in the way of time. The degree he could fail but not the mission, and he could sense that hanging around with Alfonso et al. may not yield the sexual fluid given the paucity of his Spanish, since if he was to secure a sexual encounter it would be on account of his wit and profundity and probably not his looks (despite his increased muscles he still lacked sex appeal something chronic). He thus required someone with extensive knowledge of English who would pick up on his literary quotes and be dazzled by his cultural insight. What of the buzzer girl? She certainly had that pissed off, disinterested tone of a woman intensely aroused.

'Ola?' came her voice as Theo returned to the apartment block again.

'Hi. It's Theo again.'

'Look, will you just fuck off?' she snapped. Classic signs, thought Theo. The female expresses herself in muddled ways, and saying the complete opposite of what she feels is text-book. Which is just as well, because information gleaned from the text-book was just about all Theo knew of women.

'I'm really sorry. It's just that I'm in desperate need for some help. Can we speak face-to-face?'

'Definitely not.'

'I need to know where I can find English girls.' There was silence.

'I think you ought to stop coming here.'

'Is there any other way I can get in contact with Patrick?' She grudgingly gave Theo Patrick's email.

'Thanks for everything,' said Theo but she cut the connection. He headed into town, buying sweets and sitting amidst the cheese jugglers trying to sense his next direction. When the afternoon wore on he walked to the tenement building for football, which Alfonzo took very seriously, shouting when people did not run hard enough or mark their opponents. He became annoyed when an old man in a spaghetti-stained vest arrived and kept trying to score dashing Zidane goals from the halfway line. On one such instance he booted the ball so hard that his sandal flew into the room next door and Theo quickly ran in and picked it up, stuffing it under his T-shirt and telling the man it had flown out of the window onto the back of a truck destined for the impossibly distant horizon. Realizing that he could not play with the sandal under his T-shirt, Theo returned to Alfonso's bedsit feigning tiredness. He opened the door and Lioba was inside eating a quarter segment of an orange.

'Hello,' he said surprised and with a twinge of glee, which he tried to cover by coughing.

'Oh hi,' she responded, lifting her feet off the table and standing up. 'You know where is Alfonzo?'

'Yes. He's playing football.'

'Oh. I have to give some money.'

'I'm staying here, so er, you can leave it with me.'

'Thank you.'

'Can I have some orange?'

'Of course.' She gave Theo a segment and he ate it vigorously. She watched him while he ate. They stood there in fact.

'Can I kiss you?' he asked, as he tore away the last scraps of pith, the exercise and heat of the football mingling with the rich orange colour of the fruit to put him in a confident and capital mood. The idea did not repel her. In fact, she seemed to warm to it and after a moment of consideration she leaned forward, paused for moment with her lips a fraction away from his and then kissed him. His first kiss! It was good because it was soft and shy. It was good because it was loaded with the thump of their chests. No teeth-clashing; it communicated the tears of their souls through the fluid of tongues but it was good most of all because a moment later she slid her hands into his shorts and began to corkscrew his jade stalk. It took him by surprise, but fortunately his soldier was standing to attention like a Boy Scout giving oath to God and the Queen. Had he been slow, her impatience may have quashed a positive evening. However, luckily for her, Theo's weapon was eager for ninety per cent of his day and, judging by his sensations upon falling asleep and waking, most of the night too.

'What you like?' she whispered.

'Books,' he said.

'No, I mean what you like?'

'Oh. Well, I quite like what you're doing at the moment. I mean if you want to carry on doing that I'd like that.' So she carried on while he lay back and hummed the refrain from Schubert's 'Winterreise', radiant with the beatific light of companionship. With the rich orange of the fruit still emboldening his soul, he prepared to unbutton her blouse, slip off the underwear and sends her into yelps of delirium with his Taoist sex skills. He got down and prepared to do the wild thing but she pulled back, smirking, yet apprehensive, for he had perhaps been too eager to hit last base. She stood up, straightened her hair and put her blouse back on.

'I'm terribly sorry,' said Theo.

'Nothing sorry. But this become problem.'

'I think it will become less of a problem.'

'Teo, I have boyfriend.'

'Oh drat.'

'So you see.'

'Where are you going?'

'To work.'

'Let's walk.' He put on his shirt and shoes and they left the bedsit. She explained that Theo had struck a chord with her but she was unsure whether to progress into a romantic entanglement because of the temper and stupidity of her boyfriend. Theo said they could sustain a secret tryst, meeting in designated dark spots. She said that was too risky, and also that she was reluctant to get involved with someone who was a mysterious, transient outsider. Perhaps now he could love her, but it would not be a love that would last. He would leave in time, and leave her broken and wishing their paths had never crossed rather than blaze into nothingness. Theo explained this was all of future concern and the only slice of reality that really cooks is the big pie of now. She giggled at this and they arrived at the bar where she worked. She kissed him on the cheek, entered and said they would speak soon. Theo followed her in and perched at the end of the bar drinking and trying to speak, but she began pouring drinks for others and speaking to customers and only occasionally responding to his queries and ideas.

'But do you like me, Lioba? That is the only question.'

'I like your accent.' Sobering, but female attention is female attention.

'So why not finish with your boyfriend?'

'Not simple. He very angry. Also, you go and then what? Theo, I think you do this a lot.' Now Theo was as far from a heartbreaking rake as you can get but he liked the image she was projecting and hammed it up by nodding as if to say, 'Yes, I am terrible, a libertine. My soul lusts for experience and pleasure despite the sadness I cause people on the way.'

'Say, where you from?' Theo turned around and saw two Irishmen, one tall with cropped fair hair and the other short, ratty and fat.

'Look, I'm busy,' he spiked, turning back though Lioba had moved to the other side of the bar

Irish man 1:	Your girlfriend?
Theo:	No. Hopefully soon.
Irish man 1:	You live here?
Theo:	No. I'm on an expedition.
Irish man 1:	Hah. No mountains here!

Theo:	Not that kind.
Irish man 1:	What kind?
Theo:	Religious.
Irish man 1:	Sounds interesting. Like a missionary?
Theo:	Not quite. A synthesis of different creeds.
Irish man 2:	FUCK OFF!
Theo:	Sorry?
Irish man 2:	We're honest Irish workers, don't fuck with us.
Lioba:	Teo, why don't we just wait and be slow?
Theo:	I don't want to be slow! Who knows how much time we have on this earth?
Irish man 2:	I was fucking stabbed, and this guy saved me! (Irish man 2 lifts shirt revealing stab wound.)
Theo:	That's nice of him. Anyway, Lioba, why are you being frosty?
Irish man 1:	Fuck off, I didn't save ya. You would a dun da same.
Irish man 2:	But I don't want this skinny guy fucking talking religion.
Theo:	LIOBA! Stop with this torture.
Irish man 1:	He's not fucking talking religion.
Irish man 2:	Fucking cunt!
Theo:	Sod off. Who the hell are you guys anyway? Get out of my face.

Irish man 1:	Good.
Irish man 2:	He saved me! That is what happened.
Irish man 1:	I've commited sins. Sins of impurity.
Lioba:	Not torture. I don't know you even so well.
Theo:	So get to know me. I am a great guy!
Lioba:	Tee hee.
Irish man 2:	Why are you started on the sins?
Irish man 1:	Did you hear me?
Theo:	Yes, yes. For God's sake, I heard you. What do you want me to say? Go to a confessional or something.
Irish man 1:	We will not see the end of this world through natural causes but AN ACT OF GOD!
Theo:	Jeez, what started all this?
Irish man 2:	You did, you cunt, with religion. If he gives you trouble, smash him!
Irish man 1:	Porn! Porn has the power to corrupt the mind.
Lioba:	Teo, I can't keep talking so. Bof may be here later.
Theo:	Who is Bof when he's at home?
Lioba:	He my boyfriend.
Irish man 1:	I could get porn now if I wanted. Gay shit, lesbian shit, animal shit. All my friends are into it. They call me up and ask if I want to come round, click of a button and boom!

Theo: Yes, but—

Irish guy 2:   Sing long, Auld langse.

Irish man 1:   What religion are you?

Theo: I can barely remember my name.

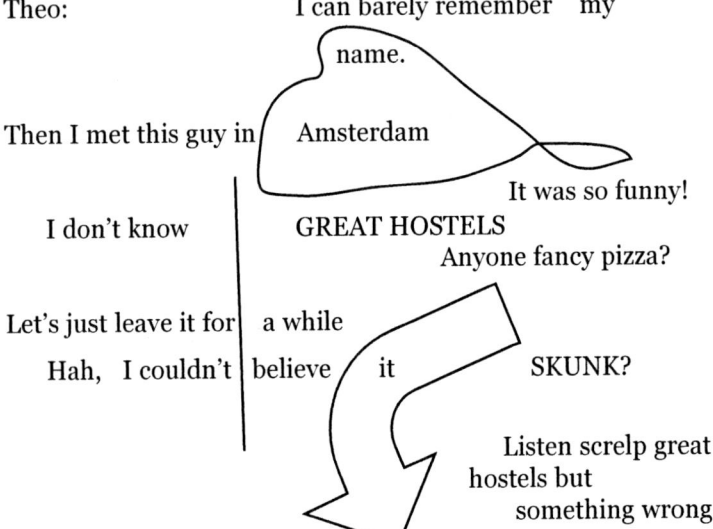

Then I met this guy in Amsterdam

It was so funny!

I don't know   GREAT HOSTELS

Anyone fancy pizza?

Let's just leave it for a while

Hah, I couldn't believe it   SKUNK?

Listen screlp great
hostels but
something wrong

That explains it!   You're spilling beer (

What?

Now listen here brother

People who don't feel the fire and guilt will go to hell

[Wittgenstein said we know what we mean when we talk, but I am not exactly sure if that is true in this instance]

Oh for fuck's sake, just forget it.

Theo stormed out of the bar, the shots of absinth making him agitated and prickly and the possibility of coherent dialogue with Lioba dashed by the disintegrating babble of voices. He swore, returned to Alfonso's and slept in all his clothes without brushing his teeth or doing his customary arm exercises.

III

The next day he walked amidst the buskers, and smoked mellow cigarettes in the afternoon. Checking his email he was chastened to see more demands for his dissertation. His degree, his MA and his Microsoft contract were all perched precariously on the edge of collapse. The magnitude of work demanded made him nauseous and so he returned to Alfonso's and watched Spanish daytime television on the crackling screen, adjusting the aerial every few minutes. As noon whooshed by he reached the most yin state and became seized.

He took out all his papers and laid them across the coffee table. There were some quotes, some sketched ideas, possible titles and meandering thoughts. Substance but no direction. 'Well dang it,' he thought, 'I'll give it direction – hammer it into order!' So he began writing up the scraps of paper and notes on the back of metro tickets while leaving Lioba to bubble and warm to the prospect of love.

Overlooking the port and lights of town, he charged headlong into a rhapsodic dissertation. Draped in a T-shirt with forehead silky from sweat and adrenaline he sought to uncover the absolute which eluded him at Cambridge, and found that it was not a concrete thought but a flash, abandoning the crystal of unity for the shuttlecock of 'things as they are' (the virtue of the small). Reverence blew around his body like a solar wind, sweeping behind cupboards, over cars and sticking nowhere but missing nothing, while a steady stream of fast photons came out of his eyes inseminating the dull, inert world of tired skin and frumpy tables and filling them with animation. Now the dissertation was an intolerable mess, packed with errors, faulty statements, clumsiness and some staggeringly elementary grammatical mistakes, but there was no time to faff around with convention, and by four p.m. he had whacked out eight of the twelve thousand words and began to read over it:

> # 'Fun: Towards an Ontology of Good Times'
>
> **A dissertation submitted in partial fulfillment of BA Hons. Philosophy**
> **Theodore Socrates Fintwistle**
>
> You want rigour but I have only roses. You are expecting clarity and grace but I feel ragged. We must get back on rough, beginners ground. The house always wins. Philosophers are slaves to unity – feel they must look past the surface and uncover the essence but the essence is the surface. The universe wears its heart on its sleeve. The surface is dirty so you think the root is clean – 'uncover'. Yet purity is on top. The root is impure. Skeptics are old men – they tremble with vertigo. Straight analysis – misses the infinite squiggles and the Etchasketch – start again. Ice is smooth but friction keeps things cogent. Space and time are handy because they spread everything out but they do not point to anything –

'Al!' came Quavier's shout from outside. Theo looked up. Alfonso was still out fixing watches and so Theo opened the window and told Quavier. Quavier nodded and asked Theo if he wanted to come to a gambling and strip club and, feeling the onset of a creative dip, the philosopher grabbed a baseball cap and joined him. They hit the heart of the red-light district and entered the darkened, cool club. The bar was swanky, and dancers worked their way around and approached people at the tables, wiggling their breasts and buttocks. It did not take long for Quavier to become goat-like and randy and he raced off with one of the women into the back chambers for some Jimmy van Pokey. Bored with strippers and flesh, Theo required elegance of wisdom and watched the desperate game of destiny as played out in the casino; the sad jerky eyes grasping the flip and shazz of numbers, cards and callings. 'Our life is a ceaseless war against fate,' he sighed.

'I prefer to see it as a game,' came the voice of Heraclitus. Theo turned around and stared at him slightly baffled. The Greek metaphysician offered him a cigar, and Theo, normally finding cigars too long temporally and spatially, accepted since the vibe demanded it.

'Do go on,' Theo implored.

'The world is a game which Zeus plays. A game of fire with itself.'

'How so?'

'If you pitch yourself against the fire it becomes a problem to be scaled, a size to be reckoned. If you merge with the casino flames you become aggressor and defendant.'

'Meaning?'

'Winning the fruit machines,' and he pumped in a series of euros to the apple, plum and banana box and came out trumps. Theo nodded.

'You know, it's funny to see you here. I didn't know you PreSocratics hung out in gambling parlours.'

'Don't lump me in with that lot,' warned Heraclitus.

'An interesting bunch, though. I studied you all in my first year. Particularly you and Parmenides.' Anger raged in Heraclitus's eyes.

'That cunt!' he spat.

'I know what you mean,' agreed Theo.

'No such thing as change? What kind of half-baked shit is that? If I ever met the guy I'd give him a slap.'

'You haven't met him before? I thought you guys were acquaintances?'

'No way. I'd nail the fucker.'

'Right on!' There was a silence. 'You don't know someone called Patrick Wright do you?'

'No,' he said. Now it is always interesting to run into Heraclitus but once again Theo struggled against these digressions. He shook hands with the bronze Greek, exchanging email addresses and telephone numbers, but had to push the work and so left a note for Quavier by their table saying they would catch up soon. He hit the early evening streets feeling tense about both his academic failure and his species redemption failure and so explained his predicament to Alfonso when he returned to the bedsit, but Alfonso could not seem to grasp it. His English was elementary, and was unlikely to be able to offer help. Theo required tomatoes, fine. Female sexual fluid – he felt it should be Lioba's. There was no doubt that she had expressed very real interest and once the damage of Theo's overzealous move to coitus had healed, there was hope. Spray paint? He headed for the graffiti artists along Plaza del Casa and asked them to spray on the sheet of paper. They charged three euros. Theo paid them and returned. So despite his concern, he was actually close. His entire focus now was Lioba. With two weeks until the firefly juice disintegrated, he felt in good time and realized that he could attempt his dissertation over the immediate days whilst waiting for her to be drawn in by his mojo gravity.

Continuing his Impressionist ramble, he struggled to weave his thoughts together and his fingers took on a life of their own. With no appetite and trembling with energy despite plummeting blood sugar reserves, Theo reached a kind of otherworldly exhaustion. Works multiplied and proliferated, pages flew, an introduction turned into a ream and he couldn't keep up. Most of it was nonsense and it required serious editing. It still had no title, answered no question and resolved no dispute but was an outpouring of experience, tangents and gags – a compressed exhalation – and it wasn't even compressed, but it was quite funny. His conclusion was ridiculous but at last the bastard was finished, and he lay his head on his desk as the sun rose on the deadline day. By academic standards it was not a great piece of work. It veered away from the title, was inconsistent, rambling, overwritten and with a tendency towards the bombastic, but never mind. He bought a paperclip, bound the pages together and sent it first class to Cambridge (snobs didn't take assignments by email) with a note apologizing for its tardiness and pleading for an imaginative and liberal marker (i.e. NOT Chummy). As he left the post office his body seemed to stop working and blipped for a second and there was sharp pain in his left shin. He was tired but there was too much adrenaline in his bloodstream to sleep. He bought a bottle of wine and sat outside, pulling out the list of elements from his hemp satchel and turning his attention back to the project. The completion of the dissertation brought his thoughts to completion of the elements.

He did not want to fail Spinny, who had lavished such faith and trust upon him, yet he jerked his head upright and recalled the premise behind the whole mission. Theo's thoughts had been linear – concerned wholly with gathering each part – forgetting the entirety of the work and the ideology that underpinned it. Now that he approached closure he came to recall that ideology; that a psychoactive drug built upon the chemistry of sad, diverse life would anchor our politics and machinery back to a bio-mystical, collective unconscious instead of the disconnected fragments that our straight, rational minds mistake us to be. The compound could do this because nature itself is alive with forces that in humans become wisdom; the force that pushes birds across the oceans is what propelled Buddha to his Enlightenment, Einstein to relativity. Mind and matter flow into one another and when the connection between them is severed through obsession with the conscious self then a hit of pantheistic energy is required to reunite the poles. It was still an intriguing position, but drugs in the water? He began to wonder whether so juvenile an act could instigate change.

Theo had glimpsed Buddhism and it convinced him that Spinny was too quick. Theo decided that humanity cannot cut corners and simply glue people back to nature through psychoactive drugs. The unconscious possesses the map to return us to the womb of euphonious fuzz. The resurgence of the species to clarity and love is a rough road of tireless, clear-headed labour. We must chisel away with unswerving determination at our clunky souls without a quick fix. Political and economic systems must stem from the rich fuzz of the subconscious, accessible through long-term naval gazing – perhaps (this is what he thought now). Yet do the species have the energy for a life of naval-gazing or must we kick-start things? The degradation of organic life was strong and the doom of employment wide. Oh how sad the paling of hairs, withering of skin and unresponsive genitalia. Time! A spiky wheel of woe... step off and up, ye nymphs and satyrs. O nerdy engineers – split thy heart! Industry built to escape the Chinese truth of change and movement – the self-destructive principle, sprouting rheumatoid arthritis in the herculean. Emancipation from all this would require more than a psycho-active beverage. It involves the outwitting of the universe, billion-millions of stars and everything.

An invisible harmonica wailed and warbled into the Spanish sky, timbled and shook; eeling towards the black, the cartridge canopy, to Neptune. Theo wanted to break things and fizz out. He saw great decadence, men puking themselves, women losing life through cyclical and menstrual misery of clutzy alpha males. Life forces drained out. Children crushed like eggs and old men shaking in an epileptic panic on buses and tripping over sidewalks. Arteries clogged, dusty train rats and anorexic bats with venomous claws, the roar burning to fading in sad worn air (salt rubbed into the wound by the nest-building sparrows). Theo longed for the steady vitality of the sun – purity beyond change and heaven above water – a final state of balanced light where us pathetic chunks of entropy attain life eternal. He returned with his pounding heart to Alfonso's. Alfonso sat up in bed with a smile.

'Tomorrow, we go to tomate festibal, festibal of tomate.'

'Sorry?'

'Tomato festibal... in south... everyone throws tomatoes, very famous, girls all take their tops off, people slide in street, tomato juice all everywhere, fun.' Theo was too exhausted to argue. He was not feeling festive. He collapsed and died briefly.

IV

In 1897, two boys threw tomatoes at each other in a street near Valencia. It soon developed into a game involving several children and parents occasionally got involved. People from the local village came down some years later and gradually the word spread that this fun activity was life-affirming and healthy. A hundred years down the line and thirty thousand folk make their way to this small village whose walls have a permanently rosy tinge.

Theo was reluctant to go. He had a pounding headache and explained his designs on Lioba, but she was attending the festival and people become different at festivals. There is melting of sober concerns, a will to raw experience. Theo packed his rucksack and they hitchhiked down the coast. Every other car had a red flag sticking out the window symbolizing the tomato. The whole thing was as you would expect. Fun perhaps, but beyond the joviality of thousands of tomatoes there was not much to it. Theo kept his eye out but could not find her and as night neared Alfonso packed up his bag and told Theo they were returning.

'But I need Lioba!'

'You like the girl?' laughed Alfonso.

'Yes, incidentally I do. I must track her down immediately. I have two days.'

'We party later and find her.'

'That isn't good enough. We must find her now!'

'Not cool to be so keen, Teo!'

'You have to understand that this is no ordinary crush. The importance of the necessity of the imminence of this shag I cannot overstate. I understand you are a very floaty and cocky young man who leaves everything to take shape and does not worry too much about times, and it is to your credit, but I have to set off now and find her. She could be anywhere! You can go home if you want, but I must press on.'

'I cannot leave. You not speak Spanish enough. I know where she is –later festival party in small village north. No panic. Go on for some few days.'

'Are you sure?'

'Yes. Esyat – small place called Esyat. Hippies and thing. Luc there.'

'How do we get there?' queried Theo. Alfonso stuck his thumb up. 'Come then, let's go.'

Theo did not want to hoodwink Alfonso into anything and was happy to go alone. He needed to be headstrong about this for the good of the world, yet whilst getting to the festival had been a breeze few cars were going to Esyat. The only other hitchhiker was a ragged waif of a woman called Irena who wore a Day-Glo handkerchief around her head. After some dialogue, Alfonso managed to extrapolate scraps of information. She said the after-festival festival was called 'The Rainbow Gathering' where naked people with dreadlocks run around hugging the great Mother rubbing half-cooked lentils over their knobs. Whilst she was informed, Alfonso was reluctant to team up with her since larger groups have lower chances of hitching rides, but she was a woman which made them look less suspicious and she knew the destination, whereas Alfonso had only general ideas of where Esyat was exactly. There were few cars around as night fell, and Alfonso was peeved because he had planned to sleep in a B&B and set off in the morning, yet the time constraints on Theo forced them to hurry. Lioba's sexual fluid was all that stood between him and the redemption of the species, and the thought was not, of course, unappealing to him on a more personal level, and despite the two hungry failed hours of road-side pleading he remained firm, fixing his mind with scholastic fixity on Lioba's behind.

Irena, however, turned out to be a tragic drunk – an alcoholic in the badness. Theo bought her a couple of beers and she started trembling and as her tremble increased she wept. They hitched their first ride from a couple of born-again Christians who took them to a campsite off the main road to rest for the night. Not ideal but it seemed the best idea since there were few cars travelling at that hour. The car pulled up, they took out their bags and ignoring the entrance fee set up camp near a multi-storey camper van from Scandinavia overlooking a lake with a pebble shore. Theo went to a parade of shops and bought baked beans, bacon and instant coffee. Irena asked him if he could buy her some beers and Theo said 'no' but she pleaded. She was becoming irate and Theo's nerves were frayed and he wanted her to shut up so he headed back and bought her two. Alfonso stared towards the lake while Irena sang to herself like some low Ophelia.

Theo returned and suggested they make a fire and Irena and Alfonso agreed. They collected firewood and kindling and constructed it using the remainder of Alfonso's matches to light it. Theo spread his dinner jacket out to protect the fire. Alfonso blew gently underneath and Irena lit the matches. Once it came on strongly Theo took out some more Ghanaian weed and they began chatting idly. At two a.m. Irena sang to herself while Alfonso cooked up the bacon on her camping stove. Theo poked the fire occasionally and smoked cigarettes and told jokes. Not long after, they became sleepy and Irena was the first to go out and was shivering. Theo put his dinner jacket over her and then lay back on the stony beach. The sleeping bag Alfonzo lent him was comfortable. A jumper acted as a pillow and his feet were a little chilly with the hole in his shoes but never mind.

Theo awoke early and pulled on his army trousers, washing his face in the lake and cooking up the remainder of the beans and bacon with a pot of strong coffee. Alfonso and Irena slept. Eating the last of the raisins, Theo prayed for acceleration and woke the two of them as the sun rose. Seconds after waking Irena asked Theo if he could lend her some money for beers. Theo said 'no' and she wept and said she needed one or she would be sick and die. As she went to the stalls to buy them, Alfonso requested they abandon her and travel alone. Theo said they could not leave her since she was broke and drunk with no food and that trajectory cannot last long. Alfonso said she was becoming too much. Theo was introspective. 'Perhaps I should just get over to the Barcelona red-light district and be done with all this?' he thought. Yet Spinny was adamant that the sexual fluid should be vibrating with emotional intensity, and no hooker would be enamoured with Theo. He would be just a client and the ether could not be charged with apathy. That could serve to exacerbate the depleted sickness of the modern soul rather than transform it into vibrancy. Only Lioba would be true – it had to be her.

Alfonso and Irena lifted their gear and headed out to the main road to begin hitching while Theo logged into the email at the campsite's internet café for the last time before returning to Ithaca, hoping his thesis had arrived at Cambridge and wondering whether it had been met with gasps of incredulity. His in-box flashed. He did have an email from the Philosophy Department. It read:

Very funny, Theo. Now where is your dissertation?

Alfonso shouted as a car pulled up, so Theo logged out and ran across the road into the wagon. As they drove and listened to the radio, Theo envied the sweet people heading to the beach for a day out in their own car with money, food and a house. Their lives were organized, rooted. Theo had no such luxuries. For weeks now he had grabbed any shelter he could and annihilation hung over him like a shadow.

He was disappointed but not surprised that Cambridge had rejected his work. It confirmed the termination of his degree and computer manual career. It was a tragedy, no doubt, which further underlined the importance of this mission. If emancipation was to fail and his degree thrown to the coffers then he would have good reason to consider the last few months a botch-job. The family took them along the main road and they looked at the meadows etc. and were dropped off at a petrol station.

There were other hitchhikers on the pavement and they lent Alfonso cardboard and a pen and Irena wrote the destination down to hold out to prospective cars. The wait was tiresome but Theo felt the cogs of synchronicity shift into gear, as though news of the failed dissertation had reached the cosmic control room and they responded with a stroke of glory to keep his fortune balanced (Camus: 'You are never completely unhappy'). His simultaneous authenticity and desperation was evident to the ether because after three testing hours of heat and hotdogs a fluorescent van with international flags a-waving screeched to a halt. The profligate Neal Cassady sat at the helm and he too was heading for the rainbow festival with enough benzedrine on board to make Pablo Escobar think twice.

V

The journey was one of inner and outer acceleration and Theo could not remember much of it, but after fussing through streets and fending off the police they reached the bastard thing; an outdoor gathering of bonfires and marijuana. Old naked men stirred cauldrons of lentil stew with their willies dangling around, and a great many people who couldn't play the bongos were there playing the bongos. People were freaking out and having sex. Nutters – the strangest and most unemployable people of Europe – were assembled together and playing games. Peculiar Irish storytellers wandered around and cheap, badly tuned guitars were being strummed by people singing Dylan.

Theo had no time to indulge in the ecological utopia and commenced his search for Lioba but she was nowhere to be seen in the many bodies. Theo found a respectable-looking old man near the shit-pits cooking up some soup in his van and explained to him their situation. He just mumbled and sang and cooked his soup. Theo explained about Irena, their poverty and his mission, but the man was a spiritual guy above the problems of the world. He just kept saying Zen jokes. Theo soon found out that almost everyone behaved like this. All of them whispered about Oneness but no one could help Irena, the poor woman, or Theo.

People milled around in a circle waiting for lunch, which arrived at three o'clock. The food was brought out in cauldrons and taken to the middle, and then one man instigated a song called 'Let the Way of the Heart Shine Through'. Theo was touched, for this primal show of tits, balls and shit was a nice balance in this abstract, neutral age. It was soon dark and some people were elsewhere on the camp or lying down. Theo strained his eyes, which had once been pretty astute with all his carrot-eating, but the unhealthy foods of recent weeks had weakened his faculties and he could not see her.

Theo had until midnight. He struggled to find someone sincere and helpful amidst all these foggy stoners and settled on a naked man sitting on his own. He looked like Arnold Schwarzenegger might look if he was quite thin, Samoan looking and with a William Dafoe chin. Theo asked him if he had any weed by way of ice-breaking and he said 'Do you see any pockets?' and then chuckled to himself.

'Who runs this shindig?' asked Theo.

'I do,' he said. Theo explained his predicament and the fellow listened and nodded but had not seen her. Theo asked if anyone was returning to Barcelona, since a straight return was as important as the collection of the fluid, and the chap said there was one van leaving at nine from the elm tree exit. Theo shook his hand.

The bus was good news but the nausea of the past weeks would be for nothing if he could not find Lioba. Like a delicate and drying flower, the future of humanity would perish without those nourishing teardrops of the female soul. He wept and could not recall which parts of the festival he had checked. People kept moving so sometimes he saw the same person twice and approached them both times. People were bumming out at Theo. Soon night would fall, and in darkness he would never find her. It was seven p.m. He heard a shout and turned around but it was just an acid head freaking out – 'I'm falling! I'm falling!' – people gathered around and gave him a group massage.

The van was returning to Barcelona in two hours. That very night was coming around after the fading day, the firefly juice was soon to perish and the journey back was three hours straight if he got a lift straightaway, which meant he had to leave even earlier, by nine p.m. latest. Tearful, he pointed his gaze up to a little crevice and saw Lioba, breasts yearning towards the dying sun. Theo ran up at speed, cutting his foot on a piece of glass but not noticing. Blood gushed out as he climbed up to the crevice.

'Please make love to me, Lioba!' he shouted as he scaled the cliff. 'The welfare and evolution of the human race depends upon your consent!' She smiled.

'Hi, Teo!'

'No, let's go.'

'Teo, I did not know you were coming.'

'I've traversed a great distance to be here with you. We have business to take care of.'

'Your foot! What has happened to your foot?'

'Never mind.' She looked down.

'But, my boyfriend. My boyfriend is here.'

'He's here?'

'Yes.'

'Forget him! I'm leaving tonight.' (If only it was raining heavily, he thought. Somehow the proposition demanded heavy rainfall.)

'Oh Teo! You are so funny,' she giggled, slapping his face gently. Looking around to check Bof wasn't nearby, she agreed and they went off. They found a small clearing here or a shrub there, but people kept walking past them and commenting. Theo had to concentrate on his skills without distraction so they moved into the distance and found a dark, cool cave with a sandy base.

They lay down with their cheeks warm and flushed with the butterfly circus of tummies. A rave commenced in Theo's core area and his white tadpoles must have been snorting amphetamines of regal standard judging by the velocity of their jiggle-boogying. Lord only knows what bass-driven music was playing out of the subwoofer speakers down below! Her love-snatch too was beginning to quiver at the glory of his rising yang. He kissed the milky soft-beige of her thigh and, ripping off his t-shirt, got ready to do the wild thing. Her skirt departed with a crackle of static and a whoosh of air, mingling with their impassioned breath.

They were unrestrained in the openness of air, her knickers and his army trousers thrown off and landing on the branches of three entwined olive trees. At speedy pace they swirled and rolled with clothes and limbs tangled in one stretching fondle. He removed her silken undergarments to reveal a beautifully snipped plumage. A real one! He squeezed his perineum.

Arching back like a jet-black cat, she breathed an Indian monsoon and ruffled his hair. Theo employed all the skills and touches he had studied including; moistening the tiger's eye, swirling the earth essence and poking the fire. He darted athletically, his thumbs awakened her meridians and his own microcosmic orbit activated. Finally the moment had arrived and his performance was turning platinum so while she lay back and gazed heavenwards marvelling at Theo's masterful touch, he took out the patch of blotting paper from his nearby trouser pocket and stole a quick swipe. If he was worried about failing to coax the fluid his mind was now at rest as the turbines of the life waters burst into the love shuttle. Theo could have done with a snorkel down there!

The act of cosmic fusion began, with their chakras

'Omming' something mad. Their two bodies dilated in a single throb with deep sighs and high-pitched squeaks over noisy breathing. They did all the positions from Theo's sex manual including; the black bee, the mare, the swing, the cobra, and even the double-jointed walrus, which is one they made up spontaneously. Finally, his microcosmic orbit about to blow and his conkers heavier than watermelons, Theo realized his moment had come, and in a volcanic explosion of chi a notch down from the Big Bang his soul-essence rocketed forward in a ten-foot jet of ecstasy. The moles on his bottom sang in unison, a marching band of soldiers whirled around his heart playing Fuzzy Warmth in E major and he filled her compassionate womb with the pale moon-juice of creation.

A moment of silence hung in timeless space as his soul swooped like a condor towards the Peruvian sunset. She kissed him, lips clammy with the sweat of love as their après-orgasm mind-bodies drifted like a feather in the calm breeze and came to rest at the bottom of the lazy abyss of Tao oblivion. They lay dazed, stroking one another and making frivolous remarks. 'You came quite a lot!' whispered Lioba.

'I know,' said Theo, puffing his chest out. 'I eat a lot of walnuts.' She giggled and reclined in the warm evening air; time for football in the park, ice cream and opening doors. Resting back on the cracked tree trunk, Theo stroked his seven chest hairs and sighed with a mellow peace.

'Ah,' he whispered. 'Fret ye not. Rest now, sad elves. There is no excuse for a crinkled brow.'

'What?' said Lioba, but Theo said, 'Never mind, darling'. It was his first physically actual encounter with those mystical beings, and it felt ace to get his pecker into combat at last. The existential tension of his life dispersed and now his spirit returned to its soft, yin beginning.

Aye, gorgeous feelings and more, but time was short and duty called, so as Lioba snoozed in animal gladness Theo rose and fastened his army belt. Not wanting to disturb her dozing, he scribbled a short note with his emergency pencil.

> Our time was sweet but the curtain of night draws and though I long for the rhythm of a domestic life I will remain always, like Tolstoy, a wandering misfit. Like a stallion, my soul yearns for pastures new and the Great Russia. Perhaps in another time we could have aged together with children and our own garlic – but not now.
>
> I shall never forget you, though, for you have taught me something, Lioba. Science may be digital but the heart is analogue. This hazy mist of aching desire can never be subjected to the autism of logic. Yet nay, the time is out of joint. The world is too much with us!
>
> Yours sincerely, The Crucified, Dionysus – Theo.

He kissed her forehead and strode to Alfonso who was waiting by the elm tree. Alfonso wanted to stay with Luca for a few days but Theo said he had to return so Alfonso handed him the key to his apartment and told him to leave it by the back door. Theo thanked him and Alfonso said, 'No problem.' The Englishman turned, ran up the path and chased the Barcelona-bound van as it bobbled down the dusty highway.

It had all worked out perfectly, and Theo reclined inside the back of the van and drew with his emergency pencil the big and quivering sun; scarlet rays zooming across inertia. Oaks and fields co-rolled into the distance over the earth and the dark blue while silver shards of glass cut the sky as the planet tipped towards the fountain pen stain of night. Yoghurt pinks splashed with angelic white against spinach green and raspberry Nashville ice cream all melting down the lens of his eyes – a scene populated with bottle tops, scratched coins, broken key rings and exhaust pipes – aluminium baked bean cans. Diesel slicked across the sky. BANG! He dedicated the sketch to the thumbs-up spirit of the cosmos, the benevolent conspiracy of stars.

A faint but coherent path dotted with blips of luck had led him through cold and hostile winds and back to America. Rammed with the verve of a rainbow and the focus of a snowflake, he was returning to wipe away the tears of the sad globe with his mandolin polisher. Armed with a snorkel and fins he had fathomed the depth of human loss and would go on to banish gloom with a semi-quaver. To fill his lungs with fumes and jimson mist. To have regrets and be young in collusion with attractive women. To cast off his muddy worries like a cobra and slink into higher incarnations. To expand his consciousness for $5 a pop. To pace the million side-streets in an old sandal treading near roaring traffic and beneath blue lights. His grammarian soul had curved into a yanged-up dogma-flipping mojo-whisky that would whistle over the drudgery of creaking bones to illuminate, to beatify.

The van tumbled through road and field and the velocity twirled his heart into a pencil feeling. He was a force of expansion in a shrunken age, a bicycle pump whooshing pink air of love into the modern heart to restore the round bounce to that most terribly wrinkled of balloons. Misery may becloud his parade. It may turn pink air of love into mouldy poo of death, but he would puff more pink air of love back in. Like a dried chickpea his soul was imperishable. Theo Fintwistle, once so pale and palpitating, had grown, transformed into a man of Nietzschean proportions. Time was his motorbike, space was his tennis court and risk was his cigar.

Printed in the United Kingdom
by Lightning Source UK Ltd.
114798UKS00001B/70-123